For Peyton, true love is worth any risk.

"I've had lots of time to think about the two of us, and I have a few things to say," he said.

Katie's heart beat wildly against her chest. For the first time since she came outside, she was glad for the blackness of night.

Peyton continued. "First, I love you and nothing is going to change that. Second, I'm as pigheaded and stubborn as you are." Katie smiled in the dark. "Third, I want to force Lone Eagle's hand on this. I think we can make him state his intentions about you. It's risky, but I can't expect you to marry me until I know you are free to be my wife."

Katie said nothing while she reflected upon Peyton's words. "What do you suggest?" she finally asked.

"Let's announce our engagement," he said in one breath. "The Kiowa is here; he said he needed to purchase provisions. We can be certain the message will get back to Lone Eagle."

"What if he orders you killed?" Katie asked quietly.

"I'll risk it."

DIANN MILLS lives in Houston, Texas, with her husband Dean. They have four sons ages 18 to 23. She wrote from the time she could hold a pencil, but not seriously until God made it clear that she should write for Him. After three years of serious writing, her first book *Rehoboth* has been published. Other publishing credits include magazine articles and short stories, devotionals, poetry, and internal writing for her church. She is an active church choir member, leads a ladies Bible study, and is a church librarian.

Rehoboth

DiAnn Mills

Heartsong Presents

A note from the author:
*I love to hear from my readers! You may correspond with me
by writing:* **DiAnn Mills
Author Relations
PO Box 719
Uhrichsville, OH 44683**

ISBN 1-57748-404-5

REHOBOTH

Cover illustration by Lauraine Bush.

PRINTED IN THE U.S.A.

one

The soldier scanned the horizon line of the Davis Mountains where the sharp peaks reached above the clouds and appeared to hold up the sky. His eyes trailed downward to the oak, juniper, and pinion pines that covered the high terrain and provided easy coverage for raiding Indians. Apache, Kiowa, and Comanche war parties easily moved about in Limpia Canyon, and too often they were not seen as they climbed the canyon walls enclosing Fort Davis. From his lookout point, Sergeant Peyton Sinclair scrutinized every waving bush and cottonwood for signs of hostile Indians. A deer leaped across a blanket of moss and wildflowers, and quail dressed in mottled black plumage skirted skyward in a rhythm of their own.

Peyton wiped the sweat stinging his eyes and noted something moving across the valley floor. He focused his binoculars on an object heading directly toward the fort.

"Hey, Miles, I believe we have company," Peyton called to another soldier several feet away. He lifted his cap and raked his fingers through sandy-colored hair.

"Comanche?" Miles asked, spitting tobacco with his question.

"Can't tell," Peyton said, replacing his cap and lifting up his binoculars. "But it definitely looks like a pair of spotted horses." He whistled sharply.

"What is it?" Miles asked.

"It's a lone wagon, and the driver is either a blond Indian or a white woman dressed in Indian clothes," Peyton observed, his eyes glued to the wagon.

"I think the heat has finally gotten to you," Miles said, squinting to take a better look. He hesitated while his eyes studied the object. "You might be right, Sergeant."

"Of course, I am. It sure looks like a woman. . .I wonder what's in the back of that wagon."

Miles turned his attention to the soldiers stationed near the gate. "Wagon heading this way, and it's weighed down with something. Don't know whether the driver is Indian or white. This might be an attack."

Peyton and Miles watched the wagon creep forward until they determined two spotted horses pulled a heavily laden buckboard. A young white woman held tightly to the reins.

"Who goes there?" Peyton called from his stance atop the gate wall. A handful of soldiers dutifully positioned themselves, ready for a confrontation.

The young woman pulled the buckboard to a halt and lifted her tanned face to Sergeant Peyton Sinclair. She wore a buff-colored Comanche Indian dress decorated with colored beads of royal blue and red. Blond hair, a shade lighter than her dress of fringed deerskin, hung loosely around her shoulders. Peyton saw she looked no older than sixteen or seventeen. A rifle barrel lay sealed in the palm of her right hand, and Peyton took heed of her finger resting near the trigger.

"Katie Colter, sir, Jeremiah Colter's daughter," Katie said. "I've come to see Colonel Ross and speak with Seth and Mary Colter."

"What's in the back of your wagon?" Peyton demanded.

Katie reached behind her and tugged at an Indian blanket covering a trunk, a few deer skins, and buffalo hides. "All my belongings, sir."

"Where's your father?" Peyton asked curtly.

"He died nearly a week ago," Katie said.

Peyton Sinclair ordered the gate open, and Katie drove the wagon through the gates of Fort Davis. All the strain of the past week seemed to hit her straight on. The past few days were a fog. She seemed frozen in the moment when she had watched her father die.

She remembered listening to Jeremiah's labored cries. Sometimes she sat listening to his meaningless words; other times she needed to bathe his feverish body or force a bit of broth through parched lips. Since her father's death, silence, deafening, heartbreaking silence, met her ears, and Katie couldn't force the reality of his death from her thoughts. The Great Spirit spoke through the wind rustling among the trees; she believed Jeremiah Colter now lived in the spirit world of the great Comanche Indians.

Moments before his death, Jeremiah Colter had summoned enough strength to speak to his daughter.

"I want you to leave the Indian village," he said.

"Why?" Katie asked. "This is my home."

"Your home is with the whites, not here among the Comanches. Go to Fort Davis now, before I die. This is not a fittin' place for a woman. Your uncle Seth and aunt Elizabeth will provide a home for you. Take the deed to the land and present it to Colonel Ross. He'll know what to do with it. Promise me you will do as I say." Jeremiah opened his eyes and captured the gaze of his grief-stricken daughter.

"I promise, Pa, but you aren't going to die," Katie said. "Just rest and soon you will be well."

"Katie, I know the Spirit calls me home, and there are things I need to tell you. Find your *rehoboth* at the fort. God does not abandon His children."

"Which spirit do you mean, Pa?" Katie thought he referred to the Great Spirit, because he seldom mentioned the God of her mother.

"The one true God, God Almighty, and in Him you should place your trust," Jeremiah whispered. Katie thought his words were a result of the raging fever since he spoke of things she didn't understand.

"What is *rehoboth*?" Katie asked confused. She had never heard the word before.

Jeremiah parted his lips to speak, but he drifted off into

unconsciousness and never uttered another word. Whatever Jeremiah wanted her to find at Fort Davis, Katie didn't need.

Katie desperately wanted to remain with her Indian family and friends. The old woman, Desert Fawn, loved her and wanted her to stay. Katie had dreamed of becoming Lone Eagle's wife, but that must be forgotten.

Katie trembled angrily in remembrance of Jeremiah's suffering and death. Where was this God when her father died? Repeatedly she asked herself the same questions. How did Jeremiah's God expect her to live without a mother or a father? How could God do this to her? He must surely be a cruel spirit. Comanche gods would not have allowed this to happen. Jeremiah should have called out to them; their medicine was good.

Only strangers lived inside Fort Davis—strangers and the white soldiers. She did know Seth and Elizabeth Colter, but it had been seven years since she'd last seen them. Jeremiah saw no purpose in visiting Fort Davis or his brother and wife. He had everything he needed at the Indian village and did not require any aid from the soldiers or other white folks. When her own father refused the white man's ways, why should she leave her Indian family to live among them?

Katie handed the reins to the muscular soldier who first questioned her.

"I'm sorry about your pa," Sergeant Sinclair said. He looked into a pair of jade green eyes. They appeared devoid of light, projecting only a dismal cloud of sadness. "Are you all right, Miss Colter?"

"Yes, I believe so. I'd like to see Colonel Ross," she said quietly. "Can you tell me where to find him?"

"I can take you to him, but first can I get you some water or something to eat? You look real pale," the sergeant said.

"No, thank you, sir. I have to see the colonel." Katie fought the blackness threatening to overcome her. She felt tired and weak, or maybe the weakness came from not eating or sleeping. Katie hadn't been able to tend to either one. Food didn't sit well in her stomach and rest escaped her.

The sergeant reached to help her down from the buckboard, but she ignored his gesture and climbed down alone. Wordlessly, she followed him past a row of decaying huts and rough, dark stone buildings with grass-thatched roofs to a small log cabin. Katie noticed several cracks caused by warped wood and envisioned the West Texas wind blowing throughout the inside. Waving strips of dirty white cotton cloth served as window coverings that did little to keep out the elements.

The sergeant knocked and disappeared inside. Katie waited, acutely aware of the gnawing discomfort in the pit of her stomach and the exhaustion that threatened to flood her body. Soldiers and civilians stared at her curiously, some with contempt. She blinked and turned her face from their view. Perhaps the conversation with Colonel Ross wouldn't take too long, and then she could visit with Seth and Elizabeth. Surely her aunt and uncle would allow her to eat and rest, even if they didn't want her to permanently stay with them.

Katie observed the fort's gate as it closed behind her. Familiar surroundings would have offered hope and compassion in her time of grief, but not these strange people living within the perimeters of the fort. *Why do I feel like my whole life has ended?* she asked herself. *Everything beautiful and purposeful is gone forever. Will this ache for Pa ever go away?*

Now Katie understood why Comanche women cut themselves when they lost a loved one. If Katie thought it would lessen her pain, she would gladly use the knife tucked inside her dress.

The soldier stepped from Colonel Ross's office and interrupted her thoughts.

"Miss Colter, the colonel will see you now," the sergeant

informed her. "I'll wait outside until your business is finished. Pardon me for not properly introducing myself; my name is Sergeant Sinclair, Peyton Sinclair."

Katie nodded slightly. "Thank you for seeing me to the colonel's office, Sergeant Sinclair."

"You are quite welcome. Would you like for me to take your rifle?"

Katie took in a deep breath. "I best be holding onto it myself, but I'd be obliged if you would keep an eye on my wagon," she said, capturing a warm gray gaze with her own.

"Miss Colter, I'll stand right outside the door until you are finished with Colonel Ross. You have my word."

She paused to consider the sergeant's request. "All right," and handed him the rifle.

Katie stepped inside the colonel's small office. It smelled strongly of tobacco, a familiar odor, but it didn't cause her to feel any more comfortable. A sense of dread encompassed her senses each time she thought about talking to a stranger regarding her father.

A heap of papers was piled high on the colonel's desk. He sat slightly bent, preoccupied with a matter before him. Coffee-colored hair mixed with strands of silver curled at the temples and matched a bushy, yet neatly trimmed beard. A pipe sat in the corner of his mouth, yielding an occasional spiral of smoke, and a military hat perched precariously on the corner of his desk. He wore the royal blue jacket of his uniform, but it was shabby, frayed at the seams and in need of mending. Katie instantly recognized a map of the territory nailed to the wall behind him. Her eyes swept over the area she called home.

"I hate paperwork," Colonel Ross mumbled, "and this report must go out with a rider in the morning."

Katie said nothing. She felt it best to remain silent until he decided to talk directly to her. Colonel Ross attempted to gather the shuffled papers into one single stack, but then he muttered something under his breath and laid them abruptly to one side. He leaned back in his chair and motioned for Katie to take a chair in front of his desk.

"Sergeant Sinclair tells me you're Jeremiah Colter's daughter," he said with an air of interest.

"Yes, sir," Katie said, using much of her strength to sit erect. "He died nearly a week ago."

The colonel merely nodded, and Katie surmised Sergeant Sinclair had already given him that information.

"And he sent you here—to Seth and Elizabeth Colter," Colonel Ross continued.

"Yes, sir. I came here first. Uncle Seth does not know Pa died."

"I haven't seen Jeremiah in years, and I dare say I've never seen you before. What's your name again?" The colonel leaned forward and picked up his pen. He pulled a wrinkled sheet of paper from inside a desk drawer and meticulously smoothed it out. Dipping the pen into an inkwell, he glanced up for an answer.

"Katherine Grace Colter," she said slowly while he wrote the words. "Pa died on June 12."

"How did he die?" the colonel asked, his voice more compassionate now than his earlier tone.

Katie watched him write June 12, 1857. She hesitated a moment, mentally reliving those last few weeks of Jeremiah's life. "Fever and chills, sir. Indian medicine wouldn't help."

"Imagine that," Colonel Ross said dryly. Once more he dipped his pen into the inkwell and entered Katie's words.

"I have the paper stating the land belonged to my pa, and now to me," Katie said, producing a legal document from a deerskin bag.

"I'll take care of the transfer for you, Miss Colter. The last time soldiers rode by your place, it looked deserted. I gather you two have been living with Comanches?"

"Yes, sir," Katie said simply.

"My advice is to keep that bit of information to yourself. Folks here don't like hearing about whites preferring to live with Indians. Some of them had family killed and hurt in Indian raids."

"Yes, sir," Katie replied again.

Colonel Ross eyed her sharply. "I'm surprised Jeremiah didn't have you stay with them," he said evenly.

Katie paused before she replied. "He said it wasn't a fittin' place for a white woman."

"Smart man. And how do you feel about it?"

Silence penetrated the small office.

"I'll be keeping my opinions about Comanches and the like to myself, Colonel Ross," Katie said firmly. She swallowed her disgust. "Can you direct me to where my aunt and uncle live?"

Colonel Ross rose from his chair, scraping the chair legs over the wooden floor. "I'll have Sergeant Sinclair escort you," he said. His voice bellowed out for Peyton to enter.

"Thank you for your help," Katie said politely to Colonel Ross. "Will you let me know about my land?"

"Yes, Miss Colter. I'm sure you'll make a smooth transition into life here at the fort. Your aunt and uncle are fine people and will most assuredly welcome you."

Sergeant Sinclair still carried her rifle, but at the present she had little use for it. Katie felt a natural distrust for all soldiers, but she knew his name and rank if needed. While he spoke to Colonel Ross, she noted his sandy hair, average height, and broad shoulders. Without a doubt, she could find him if he decided to keep her rifle.

two

Katie followed Sergeant Peyton Sinclair to an area reserved for families. Most of the cabins had grass thatch for roofs, but other less sturdy structures had tarpaulins sheltering them from rain and sun. The sergeant knocked on a wooden door of a cabin that stood in good repair. Katie wondered if Uncle Seth and Aunt Elizabeth would really want her living with them— or would they reject Jeremiah's request? In any case, she would return to the Indian village first thing in the morning.

Before Katie further contemplated the matter, the door opened and Elizabeth Colter greeted the sergeant. The woman possessed a wide genuine smile, just as Katie remembered. Her aunt looked a little plumper, and white frost wove through wavy brown hair.

"Katie?" Aunt Elizabeth half-questioned, half-whispered. "Is it you, child?"

Katie couldn't help but return the smile. "Yes, ma'am."

"Oh my," Elizabeth said excitedly and instantly reached for her niece.

Katie could not remember when a woman's touch felt so comforting. Many years had passed since a white woman had embraced her with such tenderness.

"You're all grown up, child. And you look so much like your mother. For a moment I thought I was standing in front of Mary. Goodness, where are my manners? Please come in—and where is your pa?"

Katie pulled herself away from her aunt's arms. "Aunt Elizabeth, Pa died a few days ago."

"Oh child, I'm so sorry. If only your uncle and I had been there to help you."

"He told me to come to the fort—to you and Uncle Seth, but if there isn't room. . ."

"Nonsense," Elizabeth interrupted. "This will be your home. We love you, and there's plenty of room for you."

Katie stepped inside onto a stone floor. The small home smelled of roast meat and bread; it tantalized her senses. "Are you sure there is room for me?" Katie asked. "I can go back to the village and. . ."

"No," the older woman stated firmly. "We have wanted you near us since your mother died. We've never known the laughter of children, and we'd love to make a home for you."

"Thank you, Aunt Elizabeth. Pa would have been pleased," Katie said, not really certain of her feelings. She'd forgotten the motherly ways of her aunt, and it felt strange to be near her.

Sergeant Sinclair excused himself with the promise of making sure Katie's belongings were delivered to Seth and Elizabeth. He would personally see to the care of her horses until her uncle instructed otherwise. Before he left, Sergeant Sinclair handed Katie her rifle. The door closed and the two women were alone.

Katie stood silent, afraid to speak for fear she'd cry. She looked around at the fireplace and the rocker resting nearby. Aunt Elizabeth's cotton window coverings were clean, and everything looked neat and in its place.

"Sit down, child," Elizabeth said gently. "You look mighty tired and thin to the bone. Let me ladle you out some venison stew."

Katie moved to the rough-hewed table. "Thank you, I am very hungry."

"Good, you can eat, then we can talk. Katie, child, you have the same green eyes and tall willowy shape of your mother. Jeremiah was truly blessed."

Elizabeth seated herself across from Katie. "It has been over seven years since I've seen you, Katie. So much has happened in your young life. We didn't find out about your mother until weeks after she and the baby died."

Katie sighed. "It was a boy, and they both died soon after his birth. I don't think Pa ever got over losing both of them. Within a few weeks, he started spending time with the Comanches. Shortly afterward, we deserted the cabin on our land for the village. I guess he became more Comanche than white."

"We always wondered why he joined up with the Indians," Elizabeth said, as though speaking her thoughts.

"I'm not sure. He said white people were a strange sort; they wanted to destroy the country, not be a part of it. I remember when Ma was alive, he worked the ground and tended cattle. He often spoke of his Comanche friends, but I never heard him say anything about wanting to live among them."

"What about you?"

The young girl smiled sadly. "Oh, I always miss Ma, but the years have left more memories than sadness. An old Indian woman took good care of me. She was like a grandmother."

Elizabeth rose and sliced a generous piece of bread for Katie. She silently watched Katie eat, absorbed in her own ponderings.

"Tell me about Jeremiah," Elizabeth finally said gently. "What happened?"

Katie finished the bread before she answered. "He took a cold that never got any better. The cough and fever got worse until he slept most of the time. Near the end, he took to talking out of his mind."

"I'm so grateful you came to us," Elizabeth said.

"He wanted me here," Katie said simply. "And I promised him."

The door opened and Seth stepped inside. Katie saw he looked thinner and nearly bald. His eyes lit up the moment he saw his niece.

"I heard that Katie had come," he said. Katie rose to greet him, and he gathered her up in his arms. "I closed the black-smith when the news came. Katie, child, you are so lovely."

"Pa died," Katie said softly, and clearly saw the pain in Seth's eyes.

"I know," he whispered and held her tighter. "Colonel Ross told me the whole story." Seth glanced up at his wife. "We will do our best to make a good home for you."

Katie would have felt better if Elizabeth and Seth had not warmly welcomed her. If either of them had any thoughts or misgivings, they hid it well.

Seth and Elizabeth shared many stories about her mother, and Jeremiah's death brought tears and recollections of days gone by. Most assuredly they were glad their niece had come to live with them. Katie's emotions tore her between the aunt and uncle who called her family and the familiar Indian village. All the way to Fort Davis, she'd hoped they wouldn't have room or means to provide for her. She actually hoped they wouldn't want her. Now that they seemed glad to see her, she felt bewildered. Aunt Elizabeth and Uncle Seth's reception was not what she expected or desired.

Katie's mind slipped back to Lone Eagle. He had worked hard to convince his father that she would be a good wife for a chief's son. Comanches didn't allow intermarriage, but because Jeremiah had saved the chief's life, the old Indian gave his permission. She hadn't told Lone Eagle of Jeremiah's dying words, for he had gone hunting. Instead she told the Indian chief of her promise to Jeremiah. Surely he would explain to Lone Eagle why she had to leave; Lone Eagle loved her, and it pained her to think their plans were destroyed.

The warrior most likely had returned to the village by now, and she fretted over his reaction. Katie knew he'd be angry, and she couldn't blame him. After all, she had sworn her love and devotion to the handsome, ebony-eyed Lone Eagle. Her disappearance would look like she had lied to him—perhaps made a fool of him in front of the whole tribe. Sometimes his quick temper frightened her, but she had long since decided her love could soften this one small fault.

Tired and confused about the future, Katie pushed it all firmly from her mind until the morning. Jeremiah always said poor decisions were made before sleep and wise decisions made with the sunrise.

❧

A week passed and Katie found herself settling into a new life at Fort Davis. Sometimes she felt confined in the walls of the fort and sometimes she preferred the floor to the straw-stuffed mattress, but Elizabeth and Seth's love set her at peace. The times when she missed the village and earnestly desired to be with her Indian friends, she remembered her promise to Jeremiah. Strong in her convictions, Katie firmly pushed aside the old memories.

She wondered if Lone Eagle had found another maiden. Many Indian women found him handsome, and some were jealous when Lone Eagle chose her for his wife. Katie simply couldn't break the promise to her father; she must learn to live in the white man's world.

"You've been cooped up much too long," Elizabeth said one morning after the two had completed morning chores. "Let's go for a walk, and I'll show you around the fort. We can take lunch for Seth and have a little visit."

Katie appeared more eager than she truly felt, but for her aunt's sake she agreed. The two packed the remains of the previous night's dinner: slices of roasted duck, green beans from their small garden, and thick pieces of freshly baked bread.

"I've got the basket," Katie called from outside the cabin door.

"Katie, child, did you forget your bonnet?" Elizabeth asked.

The young girl stepped back inside for the loathsome head covering.

"Must I wear it, Aunt Elizabeth?" she asked. "I don't mind a tanned face."

Elizabeth smiled sadly. "I know, dear, but here we wear sun bonnets."

Katie obediently covered her blond hair and tied the bonnet beneath her chin.

"Perfect," Elizabeth replied. "We'll start our walk to the left. There's always new construction going on. See those six stone buildings? I'm sure you passed them on the day you arrived. Those are the soldiers' barracks, and behind them are cooking sheds where the men eat."

As the two walked by the barracks, Elizabeth pointed out storehouses, stables, and corrals.

"And what is that wooden structure?" Katie asked, pointing to a building longer than the barracks.

"The hospital, and it's usually full. On the way back from the blacksmith's, I'll show you the colonel's home. It's quite nice and even has wood floors. I'm pleased with our home, but some of the married folks live in very poorly built cabins. And, oh my, I imagine the barracks suffer from lack of a woman's touch."

The two continued on their walk until they reached the blacksmith. Near the forge, Seth spoke with a soldier who had his back turned to them. Upon hearing the women's voices, Sergeant Peyton Sinclair turned to acknowledge the women.

"Good morning, Mrs. Colter, Miss Colter," Peyton said, tipping his hat.

Elizabeth returned the greeting, but Katie merely nodded.

"Don't let us interrupt your conversation, " the older woman said. "We just stopped by to bring Seth his lunch.

"We've finished business," Seth said. "And now we're just visiting. Perhaps the sergeant would like to share lunch with me?"

Peyton smiled warmly but politely refused. "There will be plenty of food for me at the barracks. Thank you just the same." He turned his attention to Katie. "And are you settling in to life here at the fort?"

Katie wanted to be polite. The man had done nothing to her, but his title and his uniform intimidated her.

"It's very comfortable," she said. "Uncle Seth and Aunt Elizabeth have made me feel welcome."

Katie felt his gray eyes study her for a brief moment before he spoke again.

"I'm pleased to hear a favorable report. I wondered how you were doing," Peyton said. "Mr. Colter," he directed to Seth. "It's been a pleasure talking with you, and I'll inform the colonel that those horses will be shod in a day or two in time for the patrol. Good day, Mrs. Colter, Miss Colter."

Elizabeth watched Peyton disappear from the blacksmith. "The sergeant has excellent manners," she remarked. "He appears to be a fine man."

Katie didn't respond. The workings of the blacksmith interested her more than Sergeant Sinclair.

❧

"Katie, is there something wrong?" Elizabeth asked.

Katie looked up from the basin of peeled vegetables ready for the stew pot. She'd broken her resolve to not contemplate the past. "Not really, I was remembering things about the Indian village."

"It's natural to miss your home," Elizabeth said gently. "From what I remember from Jeremiah, you've been accustomed to a very different life."

"Yes, ma'am. Living in a teepee and wearing deerskin dresses and fringed moccasins were not the only differences. My diet has changed considerably. In the summer, spring, and early fall our fresh meat was barely cooked. We had fresh berries, a form of bread, and roots. In the winter, we ate dried meat mixed with crushed berries, nuts, and seeds. Some of the things in the Comanche diet made me ill, so Pa always found something else for me."

"How strange," Elizabeth said with great interest.

"We didn't have regular mealtimes, either," Katie continued. "We ate when we were hungry, usually upon rising and in the evening."

"And did Jeremiah follow Indian practices?"

Katie wasn't quite sure what her aunt meant. "Yes, as far as I know."

"Well, I'm sure you left treasured friends," Elizabeth said tenderly.

Katie paused reflectively. "I did, and I do miss Desert Fawn. She was the woman who took care of me when Ma died. I know I'll never see her again, and I loved her very much."

"I'm sorry you're not happy here."

"Oh, but I am," Katie insisted, setting the vegetables on the floor and going to her aunt. "Life in the village. . .well, it was different than here. In many ways I prefer living here."

"Well, child, I guess it's good that you came to us when you did. If you had waited any longer, you would have most likely married a Comanche."

Katie avoided her aunt's face. She gathered up the vegetables and deposited them into the bubbling stew. She felt Elizabeth's eyes upon her.

"Katie, are you already. . .married?" Elizabeth asked softly as though the sound of the question would make it true.

Katie avoided looking directly at her aunt. "No, Aunt Elizabeth. I'm not, but Pa promised me to a Comanche warrior."

"How did he feel about you leaving the village?"

"He wasn't there at the time, so I told his father."

Elizabeth's hand touched Katie's shoulder. "Then you didn't have an opportunity to tell him good-bye or explain your father's wishes?"

"No, ma'am," Katie replied, barely above a whisper. She swallowed a lump in her throat and blinked back the tears.

"Do you love him?" Elizabeth asked. She gently squeezed Katie's shoulder.

Katie lifted green eyes to her aunt's face. She saw no condemnation, only compassion. "Yes, Aunt Elizabeth, I believe I do, but I also know my home is here with you."

"Katie, child, would you like to talk about it?"

"No, it wouldn't do any good. I need to forget all of it. I made a promise to Pa, and I intend to keep my word," Katie said firmly.

"If ever you want to talk about anything, no matter what it is, I'm here for you."

Katie paused before speaking. "Thank you. Both you and Uncle Seth are so good to me. Some of the other folks here are not as friendly, and I understand how they feel with the Indians burning their homes and killing their families. What they don't understand is the Indians feel the same way about the whites."

Elizabeth stood by patiently as if ready for Katie to say more, but she had said enough. "I'll continue to pray for God to give you strength," Elizabeth said. "If it comforts you at all, God loves all of us equally no matter what the color of our skin."

Katie turned to stir the stew. Again a lump settled in her throat and tears swelled in her eyes.

"Do you think he will come after you?" Elizabeth asked.

Her aunt's words startled her. She hadn't thought about Lone Eagle coming after her. Katie well knew the accessibility of the canyon walls. Did he love her enough to consider such a feat? She refused to think about it. The idea of Lone Eagle wanting her badly enough to risk his own life seemed incredible. But in a warrior's eyes, Katie would belong to him. Once more, Katie attempted to rid her mind of Lone Eagle and the plans they had made for their life together. Still Katie Colter missed her warrior more than she dared to admit.

three

Seth and Elizabeth Colter devoted Sundays to worship and rest. They spent the morning in church, the afternoon in quiet Bible study, and went back to church for Sunday evening services. Katie participated in church attendance but not the Bible study. She didn't remember much about "the Book" except for a few stories from her childhood. She didn't want to be in church, and she didn't believe or grasp the preacher's words.

Often Katie pondered over this mysterious Father God. She considered asking her aunt and uncle questions about their worship, except she feared they would be appalled at her lack of biblical knowledge. Comanche gods had been as much a part of her life as the Indians around her, and she didn't know which gods were the right ones. Jeremiah believed in the Indian ways, but on his deathbed he called for the white man's Jesus to end his misery. A lot of good it did to call upon Jesus; Jeremiah suffered more and died.

"Katie, may I ask you something?" Seth asked one evening during supper.

Katie sensed a serious nature to his voice and immediately gave him proper attention. "Of course," she said, placing her fork beside the tin plate.

"Do you know how to read?" Seth asked gently.

"Yes, I do. Ma taught me until she died, then Pa did my lessons, including arithmetic, map reading, and lots of writing," she said, breathing an inward sigh of relief. "And Ma gave me French lessons and social etiquette, too."

Seth crossed his arms on the table and appeared to be deep in thought. "I. . .Elizabeth and I. . .wondered why you don't read the Bible."

"Pa buried ours with Ma," Katie said simply. "He said we didn't need it."

"How much do you understand about the Almighty God and His Son, Jesus Christ?" Seth asked.

Katie felt trapped; she didn't know how to respond. She would not lie, neither could she bring herself to disappoint her aunt and uncle by admitting how little she knew about their religion.

"Katie, child. If you truly don't know God's Word, it's all right to say so," Seth continued.

Katie took a deep breath and toyed with her hands resting in her lap. "I remember Ma reading me stories but little else. Sometimes Pa spoke about God and Jesus, especially near the end. Before that, though, he. . .he believed in the same gods as the Comanches."

Katie heard Elizabeth gasp, but her aunt said nothing. Katie immediately regretted her last words. The older woman's hand reached out to grasp hers.

"I'm sorry, but I don't believe in your God," Katie said softly.

"Are you willing to learn?" Seth asked.

"Yes, sir, if you like," she replied. But in her heart she thought. *I don't want to learn about your God; He's cruel.*

"I imagine Preacher Cooper's messages are rather boring," Seth went on. "He's not the best of preachers, but he means well. I'm not sure what would be the best way to teach you about God." Seth contemplated the matter before speaking again. "I think reading the Scriptures, beginning with Genesis—no Matthew. Maybe you could alternate, one night reading the Old Testament and the next night reading the New Testament. And if you read in the evenings, we could answer your questions as you go along. How does that sound?"

"And where do I get a Bible?" Katie asked.

"Oh, use ours until we get one for you."

Katie hesitated, wishing she hadn't sounded so agreeable to learn about their worship. "I already have the Comanche gods," she began. "Why do I need yours?" She heard Elizabeth sigh deeply, but Katie did not look her way. Her eyes stayed fixed on Seth's face.

"I understand how you must feel. Everything that has ever belonged to you has been taken away. You've been uprooted from your home and told to live with an aunt and uncle whom you barely know. Now you must feel we are trying to force our religion upon you. Because we love you, we want you to experience the love of Jesus Christ and His gift of eternal life. Your aunt and I worship the one true God, the merciful Creator of the heavens and the earth, but you will have to find out about His love and mercy for yourself."

Katie felt anger mounting inside her, even though the years spent among the Indians had trained her to keep a calm composure. "Where was your god when my ma and pa died?" she asked with a hint of hostility. "I don't see love and mercy in their deaths."

"I wish I had all of the answers," Seth replied. "But God has a plan and a purpose for those who love Him. There's a lot of pain and sorrow in this world, and without God this life is worthless. All I'm asking is for you to read His Word, and get to know Him through the Scriptures."

"I will read your Bible," Katie said firmly. "And I will ask questions when I don't understand what is written." *But I refuse to believe in the love of a God who allows pain and suffering.*

"Thank you," Seth said, easing his back against the hard chair.

"I'll start tonight, if you like," Katie said. "But remember I'm doing this for you and Aunt Elizabeth. It's the least I can do since you are providing me with a home and treating me so well."

"You are a blessing to us," Seth said gently. "We are pleased to have you here, so don't think you have to *do* anything in payment. We love you, Katie, and we are concerned about your spiritual life."

So began Katie's reading of the Bible. She found the stories and accounts interesting, but remained skeptical. Questions were answered and passages reread to grasp the meaning. By the third day, she found herself looking forward to the nightly reading. It frustrated her that what she outwardly agreed to do had begun to touch her heart.

Katie sensed Elizabeth's uneasiness with her niece's belief in the spirit gods of the Comanche Indians. More than once, Katie saw her aunt whisk away a tear. Instead of asking Katie why she clung to the gods of the Comanches, though, Elizabeth encouraged her to read Scripture and discuss the verses. Her aunt even insisted upon cleaning up after supper so Katie could get started reading earlier, but the young woman refused. The evening hours offered ample time for Bible study. Katie would do her share of the work.

Sergeant Peyton Sinclair often stopped to see Seth about business. Katie wondered why he didn't tend to army matters at the blacksmith, but she did enjoy talking to him. He had a quick smile and kind eyes, both of which she appreciated.

"Uncle Seth," Katie began one evening after the sergeant had left. "Besides you, Aunt Elizabeth, and Sergeant Sinclair, most of the other folks don't appreciate me being here. A few of them have even made rude remarks about Pa and me living with the Comanches."

"Who?" Seth instantly demanded.

"It doesn't matter who. I was just concerned that they may have said something ugly to you and Aunt Elizabeth."

"Don't you worry a thing about us," Seth said. "Neither of us have ever been prone to gossip and malicious talk."

Elizabeth poured Seth the remains of the evening coffee and joined them. "What do you say to them?" she asked.

"Well, I promised the colonel that I wouldn't say a word about living with the Comanches or how I felt about them. Sometimes people's words make me angry, but most all the time the criticisms hurt."

"For certain, you are a better person than they are," Seth pointed out.

Katie instantly became quiet. "I simply don't want to cause any more problems for you than what already exist." She smiled at her beloved aunt and uncle. Their love warmed and comforted her every minute of the day.

One evening Seth questioned Katie about Indian religion.

"Tell me how our God is different from Comanche gods?" he asked, pulling a chair closer to hers.

Katie considered her answer for several moments before replying. She was naturally reflective and wanted to make certain her words mirrored accurate knowledge.

"Comanches do believe in a Great Spirit—similar to the God of the Bible, but they also believe the sun, moon, and earth have powers. They don't gather together and worship like folks here, because their religious beliefs are more of an individual experience."

"I heard certain animals and birds mean specific things," Seth said.

Katie nodded. "Yes, and they can talk if needed. Thunder is supposed to come from a huge bird and is very powerful. A wolf means something good and a coyote is more. . . mischievous. Of course buffaloes and eagles are powerful spirits and are very desirable. A deer can be good or evil, a bear cures wounds, skunks cure serious wounds, and elks are a symbol of strength."

"How would a Comanche get these powers?"

"Older boys go off by themselves to have visions about what holds their guardian spirit. Their powers can be just about anything, depending on their vision."

"Do you think the practice is true?" Seth asked.

Katie pondered his question. "I'm not sure what I believe. The Bible says your God made everything, and He has all of the power. If I say the Bible is the truth, then that would mean there is no truth, in the spirits of the Comanches. I don't want to let go of Indian ways—not yet anyway." She took a deep breath before continuing and hoped her words would convey the inner turmoil of two different worlds.

"Uncle Seth, I find it impossible to believe there is a God who is powerful but loving. Powerful and strong I understand, but it's very difficult for me to add loving and merciful alongside them. The parables and the miracles done by Jesus are interesting, and He certainly went about doing good. But if He was the Son of God, why did He walk with those people when most of them didn't listen to Him?"

"Whoa," Seth said, putting his arms in front of him as if to defend himself. "Slow down just a bit. You're a smart girl, Katie, and I see you're thinking and wondering about God's Word. Let's first talk about all of the traits of God, then you will be able to understand Him better."

All evening Seth and, Katie talked about the characteristics of a loving, powerful God. Seth explained to her how God created and loved all of His children. Even though they were wicked and deserved to die for their sins, He wanted them saved. God decided to send His Son Jesus to them. Jesus taught them how much God truly cared for them and wanted them to be obedient. God loved them so much that He allowed Jesus to take the blame for their evil ways. Jesus died on a wooden cross so people could one day live in heaven.

"So Jesus died for the people living then and now?" Katie asked skeptically.

"Yes, for all times."

"It's a shame Jesus died for nothing, because people are still evil. His bones went back into the earth His Father created."

"Not exactly. God raised Him from the dead after three days. Jesus now lives in heaven with His Father, and all who believe in Him will one day live with Him, too."

"I need to think more about this," Katie said at the close of the evening. "My head is spinning like a child's toy."

"Of course, we'll talk again. And you can always ask Elizabeth questions during the day."

Katie smiled. "I'm afraid I have disappointed her by not instantly believing in your God."

"She's concerned because she loves you," Seth said.

"And I love her. . .both of you are so dear to me. Thank you, Uncle Seth, for taking the time to explain to me about your God."

"You're quite welcome. I'll be working late for the next couple of days; Colonel Ross has need of me. I'll be praying for your acceptance of our Father in heaven."

Katie went to bed and woke the following morning with the same thoughts. She wanted to believe in God and accept Jesus as His Son for no other reason than to please her aunt and uncle. But she had so many questions. If God was loving, just, and kind as the Bible and Uncle Seth claimed, then why would He take away loved ones? It made no sense. Both Mary and Jeremiah Colter died before their time. Did they now live in heaven with God? Couldn't God have simply spared them a few years longer? Perhaps she was only being stubborn and rebellious, but this God didn't seem fair. She missed her parents, and she needed them.

৵

In the second week of her reading, Katie found the word "rehoboth" in the twenty-sixth chapter of Genesis. Seeing the word given especially to her by Jeremiah startled her, and she read it again. The verse stated that Abraham named a well Rehoboth. Slowly she read verse 22 for the third time, this time aloud.

"And he removed from thence, and digged another well; and for that they strove not: and he called the name of it Rehoboth; and he said, for now the Lord hath made room for us, and we shall be fruitful in the land." Katie closed the Bible. *Pa did believe in God, and he told me to leave the Comanches and find my rehoboth—to find my own well in the land so I would be fruitful. Pa believed God had a plan for my life, just like Uncle Seth said.*

She remembered Jeremiah calling out for Jesus to save him. Perhaps his cries were not fevered ranting, but a request for God to take his spirit to heaven. Katie felt a tingling in the bottom of her stomach; it frightened her. The sensation caused her to tremble, and she pushed all thoughts of God and His Son aside. Evil spirits might harm her aunt and uncle if she did not fear them.

❧

"Katie," Seth said one morning as he left for the blacksmith. "Sergeant Sinclair stopped by to see me yesterday. He asked if he could come calling on you."

Katie's green eyes widened, and she heard Elizabeth laugh.

"I knew it," Elizabeth said, still laughing. "I knew from the start the sergeant liked the looks of our Katie."

"It's your decision," Seth said. "I told him I needed to ask you first."

Katie's thoughts flew to Lone Eagle, but she dared not say anything about the warrior. "I need some time to think about it."

"I'll tell him so," Seth said with a smile. "He's not the only one who has expressed an interest in you, but up until now I haven't felt a need to talk to you about courtin' matters. You're seventeen, right?"

"Yes, sir, seventeen last January."

"I didn't like the looks or the actions of a few others who wanted to come calling, but I like the sergeant. He's a good Christian man and a respected leader."

"Can we talk about it this evening?" Katie's words trembled.

"Seth, you go on now. You'll have poor Katie in tears—embarrassing her so," Elizabeth scolded. "She's just being a woman, thinking things through."

All morning long, Katie pondered over Sergeant Sinclair wanting to court her. This strange notion bothered her. What would Lone Eagle do if he found out a white man wanted to spend an evening with her? Katie well understood what courtin' meant, and she knew exactly what the warrior would do. Lone Eagle would kill him.

But I'm not in the Comanche village anymore, she told herself. *I am a white woman in a white man's world. Any feelings I ever had for Lone Eagle have to be forgotten. He will live in his world without me, and I must go on with my life without him.*

At midday Katie offered to take food for Seth to the blacksmith. During their visit, she agreed for Sergeant Sinclair to come calling.

four

Katie listened to Elizabeth hum a lively tune while mending Seth's shirts. As a blacksmith, he burned holes in his clothes faster than she could keep them repaired. The sound of her aunt's voice soothed the apprehension about Sergeant Sinclair's visit that evening. Katie needed a distraction to keep from thinking about what Lone Eagle would do if he knew about the evening plans. Her mind slipped back to Lone Eagle's parting words—the last time she saw him before her father died.

According to the tribe's tradition, young couples were not supposed to meet in public so they arranged secret places for their conversing. Lone Eagle usually intercepted Katie on her way to get water. It was a trip she had to make frequently, and she never failed to look for the warrior standing among the trees near the riverbank. It became a game because he never hid in the same place twice. This time he stood straight in her path.

"Nei mah-tao-yo *(My little one),*" Lone Eagle whispered.

"Hein ein mah-su-ite *(What do you want?),*" Katie asked, pretending to be annoyed with the interruption.

Stealing behind her, Lone Eagle's arms encircled her waist, then turned her to face him. They held each other for several moments, basking in the warmth of young love. He released Katie long enough to tell her of the gifts waiting at Jeremiah's tent. Three horses were a generous gift in compensation for a wife, but Lone Eagle wanted the white warrior to know how much Katie meant to him. If Jeremiah accepted the horses, then he agreed to their marriage. Lone Eagle told Katie he would be gone for several days. When he returned, the two would live as husband and wife. Katie well remembered the sound of Lone Eagle's deep voice, the longing in his ebony eyes, and the warmth of his arms embracing her. Only his quick temper bothered her.

By now, Katie would have been Lone Eagle's wife.

Katie sensed her aunt's gaze upon her, and she turned to smile into the face of the woman. If Katie felt certain of anything, it was the love of Elizabeth and Seth. In a world where everything had been snatched from her, Katie cherished her aunt and uncle. Tomorrow they, too, could be taken away, but today they were alive and real. Today she could reach out and touch them, and their words and faces were permanently etched in her mind. Jeremiah and Mary, Lone Eagle, and Seth and Elizabeth were all those she loved, and it didn't matter whether they were in the flesh—in her heart they lived on.

"I've taken the liberty to arrange something for you this afternoon," Elizabeth said. A smile played upon her lips.

"And what might that be?" Katie asked.

"One of my friends, Martha Jameson, has a daughter your age, and I asked them to come by for a visit. The young lady's name is Lauren. I hope you don't mind," Elizabeth said with increased reservation in her voice.

Katie paused a bit and considered the idea of having a friend her own age. "I think it's a wonderful idea," she finally said with a nod of her head.

"Katie, child, you amaze me how you think about things before you answer," Elizabeth laughed and wiped her hands with her apron. "I know you inherited that trait from Jeremiah. Many times he would hesitate in replying to our questions—always considering every part of other folks' words."

"I guess I'm my father's child," Katie said simply. "I try not to be impulsive. Pa said to always put yourself in the place of the one doing the talking. If you can think like they do, then you can understand their hearts."

"And what does this heart say?" Elizabeth questioned.

Katie pressed her finger to her lips. "I believe we need to make a honey cake and dust off the teacups for we have guests this afternoon. And thank you for giving me something to think about other than Sergeant Sinclair coming by tonight."

Elizabeth talked endlessly about Martha and Lauren, their large family, and their love for each other. The appointed hour soon arrived. The small home smelled inviting with the warm honey cake and freshly brewed tea.

"They're here," Elizabeth announced when they heard a rap at the door. Katie tore off her apron and hung it on a peg beside the front door. "Martha, Lauren, it's so good to see you. Do come in and meet my niece, Katie Colter."

One look at Martha and Lauren Jameson, and Katie felt at ease. Any concern Katie may have felt about her association with the Comanches disappeared when they hugged her and welcomed her to Fort Davis.

Martha towered over both Elizabeth and Katie. She was a large-boned woman with white-gray hair and the telltale signs of hard work lining her face. Lauren did not look like her mother. She barely stood five feet tall, tiny framed, and her hair matched the color of desert clay. Lauren appeared to be no more than a child, when in fact she had just celebrated her eighteenth birthday.

Elizabeth ushered the women to their seats, and Katie marveled at the way her aunt brightened with the guests.

"It's been so long since I've enjoyed a good cup of tea," Martha said, setting the delicate china cup back on its saucer. "You really didn't need to make such a fuss, Elizabeth. Lauren and I have been meaning to come calling on you and Katie."

Katie smiled into Martha's soft brown eyes, as inviting and liquid as though pure love flowed through them.

"And I've been enjoying her company so much that I haven't properly introduced her to other folks. Katie is such a help, I don't know what I ever did without her," Elizabeth said proudly as she cut each of them a generous slice of honey cake.

"I'm just so pleased that someone here is my age," Lauren said. Sky blue eyes held the same warmth as her mother, and she laughed easily and genuinely. "How do you like our Fort Davis?"

"It certainly is different than living out in the wild with Pa. Aunt Elizabeth and Uncle Seth have been wonderful, and I'm learning new things every day. Are you with the army?"

Lauren shook her head, but Martha chose to reply. "No, we're just seeking shelter until the territory is safer. We have a farm a few miles from here, but Indians kept stealing our cattle and horses, and then they burned our barn. Luckily no one was killed. But in answer to your question, Lauren is fixin' to be part of the army."

Lauren blushed shyly. "I'm getting married soon to one of the soldiers."

For a moment, Katie felt envious of Lauren's happiness, but she elected to ignore her jealousy and wish Lauren the best.

"As pretty as you are, Katie, it won't be long before a handsome soldier whisks you off your feet," Martha speculated.

"Oh, it will be a long time before I contemplate marriage," Katie assured her.

"Just look at you," Martha continued, with teasing in her voice. "Those green eyes and blond hair will have every soldier and civilian within miles knocking on your uncle's door."

Katie realized the woman meant well. "I think I'll just wait to make sure I get the finest one of them," Katie insisted. She felt Elizabeth's hand around her waist as though her aunt sensed the turmoil going on inside Katie's head and heart.

Martha extended an invitation for Elizabeth and Katie to visit the Jameson household the following week. They could combine tea and talk over a quilting session for Lauren's new home.

As dusk settled, Elizabeth and Katie chatted about the afternoon guests.

"Did you enjoy Martha and Lauren?" Elizabeth asked while the two prepared dinner.

"Yes, ma'am, very much. Their visit was much too short. I had few friends in the village. Indian girls were suspicious of me and didn't seem to be interested in friendship. Mrs. Jameson and Lauren treated me like family. I look forward to seeing them again."

Katie silently helped prepare the evening meal. Her mind replayed the afternoon with Martha and Lauren Jameson. Both mother and daughter had reached out to her in kindness. Surely they had heard about her association with the Comanches, but they neither questioned her nor shunned her company. Katie wanted to be a friend like the Jamesons.

❧

Katie picked at the venison stew before her. Ever since the shadows of dusk had crept across the two-room dwelling, her thoughts twisted and turned about Sergeant Sinclair's visit. She wanted to please Elizabeth and Seth, but she feared nothing more than a friendship with Sergeant Sinclair.

"I shouldn't have given my permission for the sergeant to come courtin'," Seth said to Katie as he reached for another piece of cornbread. "It's too soon. Why, I don't know what I was thinking. Here you are grieving over Jeremiah, and I worry you with a soldier."

"No, Uncle, really it's all right. Sooner or later I would have to go through this, and today it has kept me from missing Pa. You were right in giving him approval."

"But, I didn't know about. . .how you were promised to a Comanche warrior," he said hesitantly.

Katie could not reply quickly. To please Seth, she ate a piece of venison. While she slowly chewed the meat, her thoughts formed into words.

"You could have decided not to mention Lone Eagle, but

the fact you did tells me you are sensitive to my feelings. You could have demanded I never mention the Comanches, but you chose not to criticize or ridicule the only life I've known. My gods are not the same as your God, and still both of you continue to love me and have patience with my stubbornness to accept your ways. I've never met anyone like you or Aunt Elizabeth. How could I ever protest anything you say or do?" Katie took a deep breath before she could continue speaking. "Sometimes I feel like a child with so much to learn, and other times I feel like an old woman with so much to forget. I miss the past, but I made a promise to Pa. If I had stayed with the Comanches, I would have learned to hate what I now love. Pa said that here I'd find my rehoboth. Without the Bible, how could I ever learn what he wanted for me? Without your gentle persuasion, how would I have been directed to read Genesis and find the meaning of rehoboth?" Tears flowed freely down Katie's cheeks, not tears of anger or frustration but of pleading for understanding when she didn't completely comprehend all the new changes in her life.

"God is working in your life, child," Seth said. "Even though you don't recognize it. Let me make this evening easier for you to bear. I'll tell the sergeant you aren't feeling well."

Katie shook her head. "I want tonight to go as planned. I can't run from people who are different, because too many folks have done it to me. Sergeant Sinclair is kind, and I look forward to getting to know him."

"You're a sweet, dear girl," Elizabeth said.

"Well, I don't think so," Katie replied. "I'm much too stubborn, and I long for the ways of the Indians. The things I repeat to you are the lessons Pa taught me, nothing more. You two are both loving and wise; you don't judge me or pressure me about anything." Katie rose from the table. "Now, if you will excuse me, I would like to get ready for the sergeant while you finish eating."

Katie stepped out into the fresh air and breathed in deeply. She didn't want her aunt and uncle to think she was anything other than a seventeen-year-old orphan struggling with a new life. Seth and Elizabeth saw only her youth and naiveté in the white man's world, but they would cringe if they could read her thoughts. Katie felt ashamed and undeserving of their kindness when she examined her own past thoughts.

Katie had considered the ways of a man and a woman and had been tempted to give up her innocence on more than one occasion.

She'd seen the scalps of white men, women, and children hanging from the belts of warriors and was never horrified at the thought of their deaths.

She believed the land belonged to the Indians, and the white men were thieves to try and take it from them.

She still felt a need to return to the village, even if it meant breaking her promise to Jeremiah.

And Katie knew in the white man's eyes she was a heathen and a pagan because she believed in Comanche gods.

Those things would disappoint the aunt and uncle who loved her dearly, and Katie couldn't bring herself to ever reveal her innermost thoughts.

No sooner was the table cleared and cleanup completed, but Peyton Sinclair arrived at the home of Seth and Elizabeth Colter. Hat in hand, he appeared more nervous than Katie. Seth must have felt sorry for the man, for he suggested the two young people enjoy the mild temperatures in an evening stroll. Once outside the confines of the small house and in the dim twilight where the two could hide their uneasiness, they were able to relax. Katie heard Peyton's voice gain confidence, and soon their conversation flowed with the familiarity they had shared in the past.

"Is life here with your aunt and uncle agreeable?" Peyton asked.

"I'm slowly becoming accustomed to it," Katie said. "Most

of the time, I have to concentrate on the fact that I am white and not an Indian."

Peyton laughed easily. "I have never seen a blond Indian before."

Katie liked this man. "It's not what is on the outside of me, but what's in my heart."

"Miss Colter, are you always so melancholy and serious?"

Katie hesitated. True, she didn't laugh as much since Jeremiah died. "I just think too much."

"I would consider it an honor to be able to make you smile more," Peyton said. "You are much too lovely to spend the hours in sadness, but grieving takes time."

"Yes, it does," she agreed simply. The couple walked by two soldiers who politely saluted Peyton and tipped their hats to Katie.

"They will all be talking about you tomorrow," Katie observed.

"Good." And in the moonlit shadows of evening, she saw him smile.

"They are probably betting whether I will take your scalp or not," she said pointedly.

"Would you?"

"Probably not. I don't carry a knife here at the fort."

"Ah, not only is she pretty, but she has a sense of humor," Peyton said with a chuckle. "I'll give you my heart, but I'll keep my hair."

"You have a selfish attitude, Sergeant Sinclair, although I will give it proper thought. What color are your eyes?"

"Do you want them, too?" he asked with another chuckle.

"No, sir," Katie said, feeling herself relaxing and enjoying their bantering. "I only remember they are soft and kind—perhaps gray?"

"Yes, gray, and thank you for the compliment. I know yours are green. They remind me of a jade necklace my grandfather gave to my grandmother upon the birth of my father."

"What a beautiful story. My mother used to tell me they reminded her of an exotic stone, I guess the same thing." Katie laughed lightly for the first time. "Of course both of my parents complained my eyes gave away my stubborn streak, 'cold as stone' they would say."

The two walked a little farther in silence. "Sergeant Sinclair, would you tell me about yourself?" Katie asked softly.

"Please, call me Peyton."

"If you will call me Katie."

"Now that we are beyond the formalities, I'm not an interesting person," Peyton admitted. "A soldier's life is long and repetitious. We begin duty at sunrise, and the day ends around eight-thirty."

"Oh, but you were a little boy once. You dreamed of things and of places you'd like to go. And I'm sure you always imagined yourself a hero."

"I guess I did, but I think your life has been more exciting than mine."

A call for the sergeant captured their attention. A soldier rushed to their side, acknowledged Peyton's rank, and then explained the need for Peyton to see Colonel Ross immediately.

"I need to escort Miss Colter back home," Peyton said. "How crucial is this?"

The soldier glanced at Katie, then back to Peyton. "Excuse me, sir, but Comanches attacked another family of settlers. What's left of 'em are in front of Colonel Ross's office. I've already fetched the doctor for the wounded ones. He needs you right away."

"Who are these people?" Peyton asked.

"The Lawrence family," the soldier said.

"They had twelve children," Peyton said reflectively.

"Not anymore, sir. There's only three left; the rest killed and scalped by them cursed Comanches." The soldier shifted from one foot to another. "Sorry, Miss Colter. I didn't mean to upset you."

Katie drew a quick breath. "Is there anything I can do?"

"Don't imagine so, miss," the soldier responded. "You bein' a Colter and all."

five

"Soldier, your remark was uncalled for," Peyton said. "You get on back to Colonel Ross and tell him I will be there shortly."

"Yes, sir," the soldier saluted. "I apologize for the remark, sir."

"Don't be apologizing to me. It's the young lady you have insulted."

Katie nodded politely to the soldier's forced retraction of words. She knew he meant exactly what he'd said. The soldier merely repeated what most other folks said and thought about her. She was Jeremiah Colter's daughter, an Indian lover, just like one of them murdering savages!

Confusion pulled and tugged at her heart. Hadn't she seen the scalps hanging from warriors' waists and not questioned how those people died? Didn't she believe the Comanches were right in defending their own land? And did she not love a Comanche warrior and long to be with him? Katie knew the answers to those questions were still yes, but the attack upon this family seemed different. How could the Lawrences have defended themselves against an armed band of Indians? A family of twelve now rested at three. She failed to see any reason or purpose in their murders. Why the bloodshed? What good could come from destroying a man's family?

"I want to go with you," Katie insisted. "I want to help those who saw their loved ones die."

Peyton stared at her oddly, and she felt the eyes of the soldier on her also. "It may be very ugly, and the colonel may send you home."

"I realize that, Peyton, but I have to try."

No measure of direction could have prepared Katie for the horror of bloody, mutilated bodies heaped into the back of a wagon. Peyton told her not to look, but when a torch flashed in front of her eyes, she looked directly into the pile of bodies to avoid being blinded. Katie's stomach churned. Terror and nausea swept over her while the image of the butchered family burned in her mind. Peyton grabbed Katie's trembling shoulders and whirled her away from the wagon.

"Let me get one of the soldiers to escort you back home," Peyton said, asserting his role as a leader. "This is no place for a woman; I should have had more sense than to allow you to come."

Katie shook her head. "The survivors—they need a place to stay away from this nightmare." She couldn't describe how she felt about needing to help when she didn't understand her own compulsion.

"Where are the remaining family members?" Peyton asked a soldier.

The man pointed to a small boy holding a crying baby in the doorway of Colonel Ross's office. Another soldier deliberately blocked the boy's vision from the wagon.

"Wasn't there a third?" Peyton asked.

"The doc is working on him. He's hurt pretty bad; don't know how he got his family into this wagon and got them here."

"Sometimes need drives a man beyond what he normally can do," Peyton said.

Katie pushed through the crowd to the children. Instantly she knelt beside a dark-haired young boy.

"Come with me," she said softly. "I know a place you can rest." Katie reached for the baby, but he refused to let her go. "Let me help you," she said, stroking his hair. "I'll help you with the baby."

The young boy appeared to be dazed; his eyes bore into the darkness.

"She's hungry," he finally said.

"We can get her something to eat. What's her name?" Katie asked; one hand continued to stroke his hair and the other rested on the baby's blanket.

"Emily."

"And what is your name?"

"Jacob."

"Well, Jacob. Let's go where it's quiet and feed your baby sister."

Jacob glanced toward the wagon, but the soldier moved within his eyesight. Slowly he relinquished the baby and set her in Katie's arms. Katie looked for a familiar face and caught the attention of the soldier who had first alerted Peyton to the tragedy.

"Can you walk me back to my aunt and uncle's?" Katie asked him, gathering up the shaking, cold hand of little Jacob.

"You're doing a mighty fine thing, miss," the soldier said as they moved away from the crowd.

"For a Colter?" she asked, and the soldier said nothing more.

ða

Jacob Lawrence, age six, and his year-old sister, Emily, were the only members of the Lawrence family who survived the massacre. Their brother Jason died before morning. No one knew how the two youngest members of the family escaped the murders, and Jacob elected to blot out the memory of the deaths from his mind. The parents and ten children were buried alongside each other in the Limpia Valley, where the wildflowers grew and blossomed each spring.

Katie found a sense of renewed spirit by tending to the children. The sadness and grief, which filled so much of her hours, vanished in light of caring for the orphans. She gave up her bed for Jacob, and Seth constructed a cradle for Emily. At night, when Jacob cried out with the nightmares plaguing his little mind, Katie held him close until sleep allowed him to forget. And when Jacob's sobbing woke Emily, Katie held them both. One night in the darkness she felt Elizabeth's arms around them all.

"Dear Lord, have mercy on these little children. Let them sleep in peace and open their eyes to Your love."

Katie felt Seth's hand upon her shoulder and heard his deep calm voice.

"Oh merciful Lord, we praise Your almighty name. We thank You for preserving the lives of Jacob and Emily. We humbly ask that You bring healing to their minds, and grant them a heart that loves You."

Katie swallowed her tears and held tightly to the children. Seth's prayer confused her. Why did he praise the same God who had brought such misfortune to the Lawrence family?

In the days following, Elizabeth beamed with the presence of youth and life around her. She fussed over Katie for the circles beneath her eyes, but stayed up late fashioning clothes for Jacob and Emily. Katie teased her for balancing both children on her full lap while telling stories. Martha and Lauren assisted in finding additional clothes and made frequent visits to check on all of those living in the Colter household. Even the soldier who had insulted her that tragic evening arrived with a candy stick for Jacob and words of encouragement for the Colters. And Peyton didn't miss a day, if only for a moment, to call upon all of them. He never came empty-handed, even though his gift might be nothing more than a polished rock for Jacob. Katie found herself looking forward to his visits; his half-smile and wit moved her to laughter time and time again. She couldn't remember ever feeling so content.

"Aunt Elizabeth, do you mind if I take the children to pick flowers?" Katie asked late one morning. "I don't think they will be in bloom much longer with the fall weather."

"I have a mind to go with you, too," the older woman answered.

"Good. Before we know it, cold weather will keep us around the fire."

The two gathered up Jacob and Emily and set out for the lush grasslands around Limpia. When Katie pointed out sunflowers in full bloom, Jacob let go of her hand and hurried to the thick of them. The women sat and allowed Emily to play in the midst of the wildflowers.

"I love this time of year, don't you?" Katie asked.

Elizabeth nodded. "Even if we know winter is on its way." Elizabeth snatched up a yellow bloom from Emily's hand. "No, ma'am, not in your mouth. I don't know if these are poisonous or not, but I'm not taking any chances."

Katie shook her head at Emily. "I'd like to make you a wreath for your hair, but I'm afraid you would eat it."

"Go ahead, she'd look so pretty," Elizabeth said. "I'll keep it out of her mouth."

Katie called for Jacob and the two headed for a patch of reddish-colored mountain sage. The little boy sat quietly and watched Katie twist and turn the vines and blossoms into a wreath. Katie sat it atop his head.

"Boys don't wear flowers," he said. "Give it to Emily." Jacob raced to Elizabeth and placed the flower ring on his sister's head.

"Beautiful," Elizabeth exclaimed. "How nice of you, Jacob, to think of your sister."

Jacob grinned, and then something else got his attention. "Look over there," he pointed. "Here comes Sergeant Sinclair."

Katie didn't quite know what to think of Peyton joining them, but she did look forward to talking with him.

"That young man is stricken," Elizabeth commented.

"Oh, Aunt Elizabeth, he's just interested in the children," Katie informed her.

Elizabeth laughed and Katie felt herself redden. "We shall see," the older woman said.

"Hello," Peyton called, and Jacob waved.

"We're over here in the flowers, Sergeant."

"I see," Peyton said as he bent down to Jacob's level. "And look at your sister." He removed his cap, and Emily tugged at his sandy hair.

"Katie made it," Jacob said. "And I put it on her head."

Peyton's eyes flew to Katie, and Elizabeth coughed quite noticeably to Katie's ears.

"Unless you have urgent business, why don't you and Katie take a walk?" Elizabeth suggested.

"Me, too," Jacob chimed in.

"Of course, you," Peyton said ruffling Jacob's hair. "What do you say, Katie?"

"How can I refuse?" she replied good-naturedly. "Isn't this weather wonderful?"

Peyton agreed and the three walked on through the valley.

"I only have a little while," Peyton said. "I have drills yet to do."

"Well, all of us appreciate you checking so often on the children," Katie said. "They love seeing you."

Peyton laughed. "Do you think Jacob and Emily are the only reasons why I visit?"

Katie felt a slow rise of color to her cheeks. Peyton glanced her way and laughed again. "I like your aunt's biscuits," he said.

Katie shook her head and wrinkled her nose at him.

"And I like her niece," he added. "She has the greenest eyes and the blondest hair I've ever seen."

"Emily doesn't have green eyes," Jacob said, obviously hearing every word. "You must be talking about Katie."

"Are you sure, Jacob?" Peyton asked, as though surprised.

"Yep, and I bet if you were nice, she would make you a flower wreath, too. It's 'posed to be just for girls, but maybe it would be all right for a soldier."

"Splendid, I'd like that," Peyton said, and they stopped there, surrounded by wildflowers, for Katie to weave a wreath for him.

"Take off your hat," Jacob said to Peyton once she finished. "Now let Katie put it on your head like she did Emily."

Katie felt somewhat embarrassed by Jacob's insistence, but she obliged. As the wreath sat perfectly balanced on Peyton's head, Jacob called for Elizabeth to come and see. Suddenly Katie noticed how close Peyton's face was to her own. She instantly moved back, and Peyton grinned again.

Katie thought how much she had grown to like Peyton Sinclair and his incessant teasing.

❧

"Are you understanding tonight's Scripture?" Seth asked one evening after the children had gone to bed. Katie had read for some time and now the Bible lay open on her lap.

"I've been reading about Moses and how God used him to deliver the Israelites from the hands of the Egyptians."

"And what about that passage do you find most interesting?" Seth asked.

Katie considered the question before she replied. "God took Moses from his home in the wilderness and sent him back to his own people in Egypt because God had a job for Moses. He didn't want to talk to Pharaoh, but God told him to go, and Moses went. Moses believed that God would free the enslaved Israelites," Katie said to Seth. "He was obedient to his heavenly Father." She closed the Bible and handed it to her uncle.

"Do you feel a bond with Moses?" Seth asked.

Katie looked over at the sleeping children and listened to the crackling fire. Her eyes searched the face of Elizabeth, who had turned her attention from sewing to hear Katie's answer. Wordlessly, Katie looked back to the lined face of her uncle.

"Yes, I guess I do. I think God wanted me to stop being selfish and lend a hand to someone who really needed it. He had to pull me away from the Indian village to help these children." Katie nodded toward Jacob and Emily. "But oh my, the burden it has placed upon you two. I must find a way to help provide for all of us."

"Nonsense, child. One doesn't look at gifts as being burdens," Elizabeth said, wiping a single tear from her eye. "All my life I prayed for children, and now I have three. Romans 8:28 says it perfectly, 'And we know that all things work together for good to them that love God, to them who are called according to his purpose.' God allowed Seth and I to love and care for three special people who needed us."

"It amazes me how your God used me, an unbeliever, to carry out His plan," Katie said.

"But, Katie child, your stating God used you says you are a believer," Seth said quietly.

Katie paused and regarded Seth's words. *I have started to believe the words of the Bible,* she thought. When did her heart begin to open up to God? Was it the night she first saw the children? Katie well remembered the hideous depredation of human bodies and the fury that burned inside her for the horrible injustices. At times reminders of Comanche spirits and gods triggered her thoughts, but she no longer dwelled upon them. Katie couldn't remember the last time she feared evil spirits might harm Seth and Elizabeth for the Bible reading. Slowly the superstitions had faded, and her mind lingered more and more upon the Word of God. Katie now scribbled down Scripture from Reverend Cooper's sermons and later looked them up in Seth and Elizabeth's Bible. Perhaps now marked the time to purchase her own Bible. A few gold pieces lay in the bottom of her trunk. She needed a Bible and she could give the remaining gold pieces to Seth. It would buy provisions for all of them for a long time.

Had she really come to believe in the same God as her aunt and uncle? Katie wasn't sure, except His ways were becoming her own.

❧

Almost two weeks later, Peyton paid an unexpected call to the

Colter home. Usually he visited much later in the afternoon, when he had been relieved of his duties and could play with the children. Jacob and Emily had just fallen asleep when he arrived. Rather than accepting Elizabeth's invitation to step inside, Peyton stood in the doorway and asked Elizabeth if he could speak with Katie privately.

The seriousness of Peyton's voice alarmed Katie. Elizabeth gave her silent permission, and Katie followed Peyton into the evening sunlight. Katie didn't question him for he looked far too preoccupied with his thoughts.

"Katie," he began once they were several feet from the house. "The colonel wants to see you, but I want you to know that you have every right to refuse."

"All right," she said slowly, observing the concern in his gray eyes. "What does he want of me? Does it have anything to do with my land?"

"No, Katie, it has nothing to do with your land. One of the scouts, a Kiowa, says he needs to speak to you."

"About what?"

Peyton shrugged his shoulders and shook his head. "I don't know exactly, and he won't tell the colonel."

"That's strange," Katie said, attempting to sort out her thoughts on the matter. "I probably should ask Uncle Seth's permission first."

"I already have," Peyton told her. "At first he declined, stating he wouldn't have you upset, then he said you should decide."

Katie looked above her to the canyon walls where attacking Indians easily surprised the soldiers. The vulnerability of the fort's location never frightened her before the night of the Lawrence murders. She'd always felt safe because of her relationship with the Comanches. It didn't occur to her that the friendship with the Indians would ever change until she saw for herself what hatred could actually do. Now she feared for all those people living in and around Fort Davis. If the

Comanches decided to attack the fort in large numbers, no one would be spared. Would they kill her, too?

Katie wondered if her white skin marked her a victim, just like the Lawrence family. The land, always the land, echoed the war cry from both sides. If only the two could compromise for a peaceable solution.

Now a Kiowa Indian wanted to talk to her. Peyton said the man was a Kiowa scout. He could easily spy for the army or the Indians, depending on who held his loyalties. Many Comanches considered the Kiowa an inferior race, and she couldn't help but be suspicious of his motives.

Katie knew others would hear of this meeting, and they would start gossiping again. She shouldn't care what anyone said about her business, except it involved her aunt and uncle.

Katie assumed that Seth originally refused the colonel's request in order to protect his niece from malicious gossip. After further deliberation, Seth must have decided Katie should be the one to choose whether to speak to the Kiowa or not. For the first time in her life, Katie didn't want to talk to an Indian.

I can't deny my past, she told herself. *I can't deny the love I feel for the Comanches or for people living here around me.*

If the fort faced an Indian attack, it would force her to decide which side held her heart. Katie despised the Lawrence murders, but their deaths didn't mean she could willingly pick up a rifle against a Comanche. What reasons did the Kiowa have to speak with her?

"I don't have any idea what he wants, but I am willing to find out," she finally said.

Side by side, the two walked the short distance to the colonel's cabin. Inside the Indian scout waited with Colonel Ross.

"Thank you for coming, Miss Colter," the colonel said unceremoniously. He motioned for Katie to sit down, and she obeyed. Not once did she give the Indian notice.

"This man is a Kiowa scout for the army. He states he has business with you," the colonel said.

Katie carefully observed the Kiowa. "I don't know him," she replied simply.

The Kiowa turned to her. "I must talk with you alone," he said.

"If you have anything to say to me, then do so in front of these men," Katie said firmly. She would not be above reproach.

"I have a message from Lone Eagle," the Indian said in Comanche.

Every nerve in Katie's body responded to the Indian's choice of language, but she masked her surprise and suspicion.

"Why should I believe you, a Kiowa?" she asked in the same tongue. "You are paid by the army; are you a spy?"

The Indian ignored her question. "Lone Eagle does not honor the promise made to your father."

Katie instantly knew the man spoke the truth. Only Lone Eagle's father, Swift Arrow, knew of Jeremiah's dying words. Yet, she couldn't trust him.

"What promise do you speak of?" Katie asked.

"To leave the Comanche village and return to your own people—as Jeremiah Colter asked you before he breathed his last."

Katie nodded, still refraining from revealing any emotion. "Is that all of the message? All Lone Eagle asked is for you to tell me of his disapproval?"

"Lone Eagle says you must return to the village."

"I can't go back; I gave my father my word to live among the whites."

"Lone Eagle does not ask but demands as your husband. Your place is with him."

"The marriage was not consummated," Katie said firmly.

"Your father accepted the gift of horses. You are Lone Eagle's wife."

"I agree; my father kept the horses. But I left them at the village with the other gifts. My home is here."

"You cause great anger in Lone Eagle's heart. His hatred for the whites burns even more. You will die with the rest of the whites."

six

Anger and fear raced through Katie's blood, and she fought hard to keep her emotions from spilling over.

"So those are Lone Eagle's words?" Katie asked coldly.

"Yes, all whites will die at the hand of the Comanches. Already Swift Arrow speaks to unite the warriors. They will be driven from the land."

Katie glanced at Colonel Ross, who did not understand a word of their conversation. She dare not turn and face Peyton. She did not want these two men dead or any of the others. Neither did she desire Lone Eagle killed.

"If I go back to him, would he reconsider his attack against the fort and the people living near it?"

"You think of yourself more important than you are," the Kiowa sneered. "Indian doesn't fight for a woman, but honor and the land of their fathers."

"I understand full well the desires of a warrior," Katie said calmly. "But peace would be better. Tell Lone Eagle, I desire peace. Tell him I will break my promise to my father and return to the village if he will cease talks of war."

The Kiowa faced Colonel Ross and spoke in English. "I wish to leave now."

Colonel Ross nodded, and Peyton stepped away from the door. Katie felt helpless, sick with the outcome of the meeting. She wondered how much of the conversation the colonel and Peyton should hear. What could the soldiers do in the event of an attack? Katie stood frozen to the wood floor. She didn't want the responsibility of knowing what the Comanches planned. . . . Perhaps if she explained part of the Kiowa's mission, reinforcements from other army posts could be obtained.

The trail to San Antonio or El Paso was desolate and invited Indian raids. This dangerous passage marked the key reason the army first built Fort Davis. Leaders in Washington knew the peril of this part of the country and believed the fort lay in a strategic position. Anyone viewing the fort realized the canyon walls could very well imprison those living inside. But this wasn't the time to debate the army's lack of good sense in their location of Fort Davis. Katie didn't have the mind of the army. Colonel Ross might have the perfect solution to ward off an Indian attack. Defending civilians and the settlers were his lifeblood. Colonel Ross's solution might be quite simple.

"Miss Colter, you look pale," Colonel Ross stated, interrupting her racing thoughts. "Shall I have a soldier fetch smelling salts?"

Katie shook her head. She must say something about the Kiowa's threats.

"Colonel Ross. Are the words spoken in this room private?"

"Yes, Miss Colter, if you so desire. Sergeant Sinclair?"

"Yes, sir. Miss Colter's words are confidential."

"Perhaps additional sentries for the canyon walls might be a consideration," Katie said with a deep sigh.

Colonel Ross sat erect and appropriately gave Katie his full attention. "So the Kiowas are planning an attack?"

Katie folded her hands in her lap. They were moist and cold, like Jacob's hands the night she brought home the children.

"Not the Kiowas, but the Comanches," Katie said, purposely securing eye contact with the colonel. "I don't think the Kiowa lied because his words held other matters of truth."

"Did he say when?" the colonel asked.

"No, sir. He most likely didn't know for certain. You and I both know Comanche warfare is in stages—circling and striking when they have the advantage."

"Why did he have to speak with you about it?" the colonel asked.

Katie took another deep breath. "I think, sir, his purpose

was to see my reaction. Perhaps Swift Arrow wondered if I had abandoned all the Comanche ways."

"And was he satisfied?"

Katie gave Colonel Ross a wry smile. "I believe in peace."

"Is there anything else I need to be aware of? The conversation with the Kiowa appeared longer, and the sergeant and I would have to be fools not to note the tension."

Katie nodded. "The other matter had nothing to do with their talks of war."

The walk back home proved more of silence than words. Katie remained deep in thought, pondering over every word spoken with the Kiowa. Granted the Comanches had hit settlers and small bands of travelers for a number of years. More than once they'd climbed the canyon walls into Fort Davis and struck terror. The Comanches, with their strategic element of surprise, always kept the army at a disadvantage. She had little else to tell Colonel Ross. The Indians had threatened to wipe out the whites since they first arrived in the territory. The threat merely reinforced all of their actions in the past.

Certainly Lone Eagle could not be so upset that he increased the number of attacks to bring her back to him. The thought hardly made sense, unless his anger and revenge lay with pride—and Lone Eagle, as all other warriors, had a great deal of pride.

"Katie," Peyton began. "I'm sorry about today."

"There's no need for you to be sorry. It was my choice to speak with the Kiowa." Katie purposely avoided his eyes.

"He obviously upset you."

"He would upset anyone."

"But why do I have a feeling the things you didn't tell the colonel are the most serious ones."

"Oh, Peyton," Katie attempted humor. "I believe you are being overly protective."

"Don't be coy with me," Peyton said. He grabbed her shoulders and whirled her around to face him. He trembled in uncharacteristic rage. "I want to know what the Kiowa said."

Katie felt her own anger race through her veins. "No! It's none of your concern, and besides, you're hurting me. Now please let go."

Peyton instantly released his hold on her as though he had seized a forging iron. "I'm sorry," he said. "Katie, I never intended to hurt you. I had no right to demand anything of you."

"That's right, you didn't," Katie spat at him. "I'll make my own way home from here, Sergeant Sinclair."

In the wee hours of the morning, Katie tossed and turned over the events of the day. First she would contemplate every word from the Kiowa scout, then she'd recall Peyton's demands. Her thoughts raced with such fervor that she failed to put either of the matters at rest. Tightly closing her eyes, Katie tried to divert her thoughts. Neither incident should rob her of sleep, but the resolution didn't stop the unrest rising and falling in her spirit.

She gave up trying to figure out why Lone Eagle sent a Kiowa with his message. Lone Eagle could very well have held the man's family hostage until he returned with Katie's answer, or he could have promised horses or rifles in exchange. Lone Eagle wouldn't risk the life of another Comanche warrior, but he would consider the job for another tribe member.

The Kiowa couldn't be trusted, and she should have stated so to the colonel.

Why Lone Eagle sent a Kiowa is not important, Katie told herself. *I want to know why the message was sent at all.*

The Kiowa spoke correctly in one aspect of it all. Lone Eagle would not unite other warriors over a mere woman. His position as the chief's son allowed him the privilege of leading war parties. If Lone Eagle felt the white soldiers had his wife, his property, then he would go to any length to get her back. Yes, most assuredly pride and honor stood as the most logical answer for Lone Eagle to demand her return.

In the eyes of the warrior, she had abandoned her husband, and the whites were to blame.

Katie shivered in her sleep. What if Lone Eagle intended to punish her? Within the tribal laws, he had the right, especially if he now considered her a slave rather than an equal. Most likely she lost any respectability the day she left for Fort Davis.

The last words Katie spoke to the Kiowa rang through her mind. She asked for peace, and if joining him at the village stopped the Indian raids, then she would return to him. If she truly loved Lone Eagle, then why did a life with him suddenly sound frightening? Was the trepidation due to Lone Eagle forcing her into marriage? She remembered how it used to be with him; she couldn't wait to become his wife. What happened to those hopes and dreams? Was it the search for her rehoboth, the special place where she would prosper in the land, or had she resigned herself to a white man's world?

In the darkness, Jacob whimpered. Katie reached up and patted his back until he drifted back to sleep. Emily cried out, but moments later she, too, rested quietly. Katie's thoughts reflected upon Peyton and his unwarranted lashing out at her. He'd been furious when she refused to repeat all of the Kiowa's words. Oh, if she could only sleep and banish the events of the day.

Granted, Katie recognized her own stubbornness, and she often refrained from revealing her innermost thoughts. But she didn't see any reason to alarm Peyton about Lone Eagle's insistence that she return to the village. Uncle Seth did know of her involvement with Lone Eagle, but she firmly believed he would not reveal such information to anyone without her permission. Why would she want to tell Peyton about Lone Eagle? It only invited more problems. She treasured their friendship and looked forward to his regular visits, but not at the expense of giving him every secret of her life. The problem lay with Katie and Lone Eagle, not Sergeant Peyton Sinclair.

"Katie," Seth whispered. "I haven't been able to sleep, and I could tell you were restless, too. Did something happen when you spoke with the Kiowa scout today?"

"Yes," she said softly. "I can't seem to get it out of my mind."

"Do you want to talk about it?" he asked. "We can go outside if you like."

"Oh, I hate to bother you with it."

"If it is important enough to keep you from sleeping, then I want to hear it."

The two silently moved outside and seated themselves on the front steps.

"What did the scout say to upset you?" Seth asked. He placed a comforting arm around his niece's shoulders.

Katie leaned her head on his shoulder. The night air had turned cool, and she shivered. "Well, to begin with, he spoke in Comanche, so that meant the colonel and Peyton couldn't understand him." Katie told her uncle only of the Comanche threat to all of the white people. "I told Colonel Ross about the threat."

"Why did the scout tell you?" Seth asked.

"Probably to see if I was loyal to the Comanches," Katie replied. "But I assured both the scout and the colonel that I only wanted peace."

"I believe you spoke well," Seth insisted.

"There's more. On the way back home, Peyton became very angry when I wouldn't repeat the conversation word for word. We had a bit of an argument, and I walked home alone. I know he meant well, but he hit my stubborn streak."

Seth squeezed her shoulders. "I'm sorry. I should have stuck by my original decision or accompanied you to the colonel's office."

"Oh Uncle, I don't blame you. It hadn't even entered my mind."

He kissed the top of her head. "I'll pray for both of you."

Peyton did not visit the Colter home the next day or the next. By the end of five days, Katie determined the depth of his anger had caused him to break ties with her permanently. She knew the children missed Peyton, for Jacob asked for him. Seth began taking the little boy on short excursions, filling his hours with new sights and sounds. She knew both Seth and Elizabeth loved the children and wanted to adopt them. Perhaps Peyton's disappearance was good for them all. It provided a way for Seth to secure his relationship with Jacob.

Katie pushed any thought of missing Peyton from her mind. Their argument proved she was better off without him. She didn't need another man to tear at her emotions.

"Is the sergeant out on patrol?" Elizabeth asked one morning at breakfast.

Seth rested his coffee mug on the table. "No, I've seen him every day this week."

"Well, up until this week, he had made daily visits to see Katie and the children, but I haven't seen him this week."

Katie felt her face redden. "Peyton and I quarreled," she said to Elizabeth quietly. "I'm sorry; I had no idea he wouldn't come to visit Jacob and Emily."

"That's all right, dear," Elizabeth soothed. "Maybe you two need time to mend your differences."

"Do I need to confront him about the matter?" Seth asked. Even the children stopped eating when his voice raised.

"I'd rather that you didn't. Perhaps Aunt Elizabeth is right, and we just need time."

"All right, then, but I have no problem looking into the situation," Seth stated firmly.

Katie breathed in deeply. She didn't want her aunt and uncle fretting about her friendship with Peyton.

Sunday morning, Katie considered feigning an illness and missing church. Peyton always attended Reverend Cooper's services unless he was out on patrol, and she really wanted to avoid him. After further contemplation, she refused to give in to her own selfish desires.

Peyton was already seated when the Colters entered the wood and thatch-covered building and secured a bench near the front. During the sermon Katie found her thoughts straying. She missed Peyton, and she did want to mend their differences, but she wasn't ready to take the first step toward reconciliation.

At the close of the service, Peyton stood directly in her path outside the church. "You linger long enough, and he'll be gone for sure," Elizabeth whispered. Wordlessly Elizabeth lifted Emily from Katie's arms, while Jacob already held Seth's hand.

Peyton held his cap in hand, and when she tried to walk by him, he stepped in her way.

"I would like to talk to you," Peyton said softly.

"Our last conversation ended rather unpleasantly," Katie said, purposely staring at her family, who had stopped to visit with the Jamesons.

"I take entire blame for our misunderstanding," he said. "Again I apologize."

Katie turned to face him. He had such a kind face, but she didn't see the familiar sparkle. She'd told Jacob the sergeant had laughing eyes. Those eyes, which had attracted her to him with their warmth and sincerity, now appeared distant.

"It wasn't all your fault," Katie said. Her eyes moistened and a lump rose in her throat. "I do miss your visits to see the children, and they miss you."

"Jacob and Emily aren't the only reason why I came by the cabin," he said. "I enjoyed our little talks. Can I start calling on you again?"

Katie nodded and felt a tear slipping from her eye. *Why am I weeping about this? It must be the warm day.* She knew Peyton saw her display of emotion, and she immediately felt the color rise in her cheeks.

"May I stop by this afternoon?" he asked, not taking his eyes from her face.

"I'll look forward to it," Katie said, hearing her own voice tremble. "Do you remember when the children nap?"

"Yes, I do, and I'll be there early. I just wanted to see you for a few minutes before going out on patrol tomorrow morning."

Katie instantly felt alarm, and she didn't attempt to disguise it.

"Is the Kiowa scout going?"

"No, he's been dismissed from his duties."

Katie breathed a sigh of relief. "How long will you be gone?"

"Three or four days," Peyton said easily. "It's a routine patrol."

"How many men are riding with you?"

"Eight others."

"That's not very many, Peyton."

"We need to keep enough soldiers here in case of attack," Peyton pointed out.

Katie nodded sadly. She turned her head so he wouldn't see any more tears, but in doing so she caught sight of the Kiowa. The Indian stood watching both of them.

"What's wrong, Katie?" Peyton asked gently. "You look ill."

"The Kiowa is still here; I thought he would have left the fort," she said fearfully.

He turned to face the Indian, but by then the Kiowa had walked away. Peyton focused his attention upon Katie.

"I would do anything to wipe the fear from your eyes," he said, stepping closer to her.

Katie avoided his gaze and glared at the back of the Kiowa. "Don't leave on patrol tomorrow. Can't Colonel Ross send someone else?"

"I have my orders; I have a job to do," he explained. "Soldiers can't choose where and when they want to report for duty."

seven

Katie trudged through the next two days, supplying extra activities for Jacob and Emily and insisting upon doing all of the cooking. She said Elizabeth needed more time with the children, but in actuality Katie didn't want to think of anything happening to Peyton or the other soldiers.

On the third day, Katie tucked lunch into a basket and took Jacob with her to the blacksmith shop. She wanted the little boy to see Seth at work, yet not be in the way of the fiery forge.

"Will you tell me a story?" Jacob asked as they prepared to leave the cabin.

Katie remembered a story that Jeremiah once told her. She grasped the child's hand and carried the basket with the other. "A small Indian boy received a spotted pony from his father. He was excited and looked forward to riding and training it, but the pony proved wild and could not be broken. After many weeks of attempting to ride the pony, the boy sought his father's advice. 'Pretend that you live inside the pony,' his father said. 'When you know the pony's heart, then it will be your friend.' The small boy worked hard and observed the animal and its habits. Slowly the pony began to eat from his hand and allowed the boy to stroke it. When the boy fully understood the pony, he no longer felt afraid of it and made friends. The pony learned to love and trust the small boy, and one day he allowed the boy to ride him."

Katie's story sounded simple enough, but she wanted Jacob to see Indian children were much like white children. She felt understanding between the Indians and whites was the first step to peace.

"I like the story," Jacob announced. "Even if it is about an Indian."

Jacob watched Seth hammer and shape white hot metal into horseshoes without so much as a single word. After an hour passed, Seth asked the little boy if he had anything to say. Jacob's blue eyes grew wide, and soon a huge assortment of questions poured from his mouth.

At noon the three sat down together. Seth and Jacob talked constantly, but Katie's eyes darted back and forth to the front gate in hopes of seeing Peyton.

"The patrol will be back soon," Seth said quietly.

Katie immediately glanced down at the unfinished food before her and felt a slow blush.

"I guess I don't hide my thoughts well," she said, somewhat flustered.

"Not this time," Seth said with a chuckle, and he stretched out his long legs. Within moments, Jacob stretched out his short legs.

Katie and Seth couldn't help but laugh at the child's imitation. Each time Seth took a bite of food, so did Jacob. At one point, a soldier walked by and Seth waved; so did Jacob.

"I believe we have a blacksmith in the making," Katie said.

"You may be right," Seth said. When she took another longing gaze toward the front gate, he spoke again. "Katie, child, I believe you like the sergeant a little more than you care to admit."

Katie hesitated before answering, as always, running his words through her head. "He is a good friend," she said simply.

"All good relationships begin with friendship, and I already know how he feels about you."

"Did he tell you something?" Katie asked, her curiosity sparked.

"Um, yes he did, and I fully approve."

"Well, what did Peyton say?"

"I'll let him tell you for himself. The question you need to ask yourself is, how do you feel about him?"

Katie paused and wiped bread crumbs from Jacob's mouth. "I'm not sure," she said slowly. "It's not a simple thing, Uncle Seth. You know how things would have been if I had stayed with the Indians." Katie glanced first at Jacob, who was listening to every word, then into the face of her uncle.

"Yes, I know very well," Seth said. "Elizabeth and I have discussed what could have easily happened if you remained living there. We don't keep secrets from each other, and we know you must be confused—not just about Sergeant Sinclair, but God, different cultures, grieving for Jeremiah, and how you feel about Emily and Jacob. The list is endless, and we are praying for you."

"Then you understand how torn I am?"

"Of course we do. Jeremiah was my brother, and I saw the same turmoil in him. It saddens me to see you in the same situation."

"How did you become so wise?" Katie asked seriously.

Seth chuckled, and so did Jacob. "I've never considered myself a wise man, but thank you. I think God gives us a measure of wisdom with each year we get older." Seth lightly touched Jacob's nose. "Much like a peppermint stick before a dose of bad-tasting medicine."

Shortly thereafter, Jacob showed signs of tiring. Katie suggested the two hurry home to check on Emily.

"Thank you for bringing lunch," Seth said. "Jacob, you can come by and visit me anytime."

"We enjoyed watching you work," Katie said. She stood, but Jacob reached over and hugged Seth.

Sentiment tore at Seth, and he pulled the little boy tightly to him.

"Will you be my papa?" Jacob whispered loud enough for Katie to hear. "Will you be my papa and not let the Indians make you die?"

Katie had rarely seen a grown man cry. Even when her

mother died, Jeremiah slipped away to weep. Yet, the tears from her uncle flowed unchecked, and she felt her own eyes fill with liquid emotion.

"God bless you, Jacob," Seth said. "I love you, child, and I'll do my best."

At home, before Katie had a chance to tell what she and Jacob had been doing all morning, Elizabeth proudly stood Emily on the floor for Katie to see her walk.

This has truly been a wonderful day, Katie told herself. *Jacob is reaching out for love from Seth, and Emily takes her first steps. What a blessing for Uncle Seth and Aunt Elizabeth.*

Katie caught herself repeating her last thoughts. She had used the word "blessing" without considering that her thoughts indicated a belief in God. *I've just been around people who believe in God, and their speech has settled into mine,* she told herself. *Or am I beginning to trust in the God of the Bible?*

On the morning of the fourth day with no word from the patrol, Elizabeth suggested Katie visit Lauren. When Katie attempted to prepare Jacob and Emily, her aunt said the children needed to stay at home. No doubt, Elizabeth wanted Katie to turn the waiting hours into girl talk. Reluctantly Katie agreed. She knew Elizabeth would have more work to do with Jacob and Emily underfoot.

The entire Jameson household, eight children in all, noisily welcomed Katie. When she saw Martha had all of them, except Lauren, in the midst of schooling, Katie apologized for the intrusion. She politely excused herself, but Martha wouldn't hear of it.

"Lauren, you and Katie just go about your visiting—perhaps a walk would do you both good," Martha urged.

Katie shook her head. "No, Mrs. Jameson. I don't want to interrupt your teaching. Is there any way I can help?"

Martha wrinkled her nose at Katie in a disapproving manner.

The gesture reminded Katie of one of the children laboring over a slate.

"Please?" Katie persisted.

Martha agreed and laughed in the process. Soon Katie sat on the floor beside one of the younger boys. He didn't look much older than Jacob, but still he managed to read a little. Katie helped him write his letters and do simple addition problems on a slate. It occurred to her that Jacob needed to be learning, and perhaps she should mention it to Seth and Elizabeth.

For the next two hours, Katie assisted Martha and Lauren in different levels of reading and arithmetic. Martha Jameson had taught school before she married and knew exactly how to assign lessons according to the ability of her children. As soon as a young Jameson could hold a piece of chalk or recognize a letter, she encouraged him to read and do numbers. Katie loved the way in which Martha praised her children's work and gently instructed those who had difficulty.

"My ma taught school before she married my father," Katie told Martha and Lauren.

"What all did she teach you?" Martha asked, stepping over to the cook fire and stirring a pot of beans.

"The same things you teach your children: reading, writing, arithmetic, geography, social etiquette, and history. She also taught me French. Ma always told me that the world was a big place and filled with many experiences. She encouraged me to ask questions and to dream. I remember in the evenings Pa and I used to listen to her read the Bible. I had forgotten much of the Bible teachings until Uncle Seth encouraged me to begin reading it again."

"Did your schooling stop when your ma died?" Martha asked.

"Just the Bible reading. When I started studying the Scriptures here, it loosened my memory of what Ma used to read. My pa had graduated from a university in Connecticut and carried on my studies, except he added wilderness survival as well as the language and customs of the Comanches." Katie thought better of mentioning the Indians, but she'd already spoken of it.

Martha instantly picked up on Katie's discomfort. "Katie, I believe you received a fine education," she said.

"Can Katie teach us about Indians and surviving in the wild?" the eldest Jameson son asked.

Martha paused a moment, and all of the children waited for their mother's response.

"If Katie is willing, she can teach you about those things, but first you must work hard on your reading, writing, and arithmetic. And perhaps Jacob would like to join us," Martha finally said. "What do you think about that, Katie? Of course, you must ask your aunt and uncle's permission."

"It would be great fun," Lauren said excitedly. "And she could also teach me French, although I don't know if a soldier's wife needs to know it."

Katie felt pleased from the top of her head to her tingling toes. "I'll ask my aunt and uncle, except I'm not sure if I would be a good teacher."

"You've been a wonderful help today," Martha said. "I believe that you not only have the gift of teaching, but also the gift of patience and encouragement. God's truly blessed you with an abundance of special gifts. Make sure you thank Him by using those gifts for the benefit of others."

Katie could only listen and show respect for the woman's words. The thought of being useful made her feel good, especially teaching like her ma had done.

Had this God really given her gifts? The thought seemed incredible that He would give gifts to someone who wasn't a believer. Katie wondered if stubbornness played a part in her refusal to accept God and His Son Jesus, or did she need some type of proof of His existence? *God, if You are truly there, show me so I can believe. I'm so confused about my life, and I don't know what is real or truth.*

Katie and Lauren finally slipped away from the Jameson household. Their time together would be short, but they were determined to make the most of it. Katie treasured her friendship with Lauren and respected their differences in personality. Quick laughter, delightful spontaneity, and an unselfish, giving attitude were all a part of Lauren Jameson. No wonder a soldier had fallen in love with her; Lauren invited love and joy in every breath she took. Katie saw Lauren generously shower those traits upon everyone she met, and Lauren showed Katie what true beauty really meant. As the two girls walked about the fort, Lauren spoke to all they passed, if not with her voice then with a nod or smile.

"Are your wedding plans completed?" Katie asked politely.

"Not yet. Mama has finished altering my dress, and I've been working on needlepoint every chance I get. Mama insists on so many things to be completed for our new home, but it really isn't necessary. Besides I hate to burden her with extra sewing and the like to help me set up housekeeping."

"I know I'm being selfish, but I'm glad you will be living close by," Katie said.

"No one could be more selfish than I am," Lauren said. "I want to be married now and get all of this wedding nonsense behind me. Mama and Papa want everything to be perfect, but the day will be wonderful with or without the finery and party plans."

"They want to give you the best because they love you," Katie said. "My aunt is always talking about when I get married, we will do this or that. Maybe it's more fun for them than us."

"Probably so. I simply don't like to be the center of attention. It makes me feel uncomfortable," Lauren said, shaking her head. Her mood suddenly lifted, and she began to laugh. "Now tell me about you and Sergeant Sinclair."

Katie smiled at the teasing note in her friend. "There's nothing to tell; we're good friends."

"Good friends, my eye. He visits your cabin nearly every day."

"To see the children, or Uncle Seth, or Aunt Elizabeth," Katie said with an air of exactness.

"Oh, you are storytelling, Katie," Lauren accused. "I know for a fact the sergeant asked your uncle if he could come courtin'."

Katie attempted to give her a surprised look, but the mischievous twinkle in Lauren's eyes wouldn't permit it. "And how did you know about such a conversation?" Katie asked.

"Your aunt told my mother," Lauren said with a toss of her head. "And some things a woman just knows—like affairs of the heart."

Katie couldn't help but burst into laughter at Lauren's dramatics.

"It's good to see you laugh more," Lauren finally said. "I have been praying for you to find joy in your life."

"Thank you," Katie replied. "Since Jacob and Emily have come to live with us, my mind has been occupied with them instead of myself. And yes, seeing Peyton, I mean Sergeant Sinclair, keeps me busy."

"He cares for you very deeply," Lauren said softly.

"How do you know?" Katie asked in the same hushed tone.

"All you have to do is look at his face; it's the same way my soldier looks at me. It gives away everything they are trying to hide."

Katie didn't want to discuss Peyton any longer. If she knew her own feelings for him then she could respond more readily to Lauren. But didn't she love Lone Eagle? She thought real feelings of love never changed. Sometimes she wished she could push the Indian from her heart forever and allow Peyton to take his place. Could it be she feared Lone Eagle's temper as much as she cared for him? Or was she afraid to let another man into her heart? As much as Katie refused to admit it, she saw the caring in Peyton. A combination of guilt and perplexity forced her to refrain from any romantic notions. Peyton must remain a friend.

The Kiowa saw us talking together, Katie remembered. *Our conversation must have looked as though we were more than friends, especially in light of making amends for our disagreement.* Once more fear and anxiety cast a menacing shadow. The Kiowa spy would surely inform Lone Eagle about Peyton.

If I believed, I would pray, Katie thought sadly. *If the soldiers are attacked and Peyton is killed, it will be my fault.* The words of the Kiowa echoed across her mind. As much as she hated to ever talk to the Indian again, she would have to find out Lone Eagle's answer. But now, deep in her heart, did she really want to leave Seth and Elizabeth? What of her promise to Jeremiah? And how was she to find her rehoboth?

The ugliest thought of all sprung from Lone Eagle's threat to wipe out the whites. The warrior didn't say she would be to blame, but Katie knew Lone Eagle. Many times he revealed only a portion of his thoughts with the intention of waiting for a response. He didn't anticipate anything, rather he allowed others to react before he proceeded with his plans. Lone Eagle had learned the lessons of cunning and wit in dealing with his enemies. Katie wondered if the Kiowa's words were intended to scare her into returning to the Comanche village.

eight

The fifth day of the patrol's absence crept by much like a lingering fever, and still no word from the army patrol. Seth and Elizabeth prayed for the men during mealtimes and at bedtime. Katie listened to their prayers and bowed her head in respect to their God, but she didn't appeal to the Comanche gods, either. A lump rose in her throat, and she couldn't eat or sleep.

For the second night Katie tossed and turned, unable to relax or pull peace from the recesses of her mind. Racing thoughts became like nightmares, and she even imagined hearing the war cries of Comanches and the screams of dying men. Peyton said the patrol would be back in three or four days; when tomorrow dawned, it would be the sixth day. If only the men would return unharmed.

Night turned into morning and Katie watched the chalky pastels of purple, pink, and orange spread across the sky. She wondered how nature could continue its unrivaled beauty and not be sensitive to the turmoil of the people around it. The Comanches relied solely upon the spirits of nature to guard and direct them in their dealings with the enemy. Whites prayed to a sovereign God to protect them from evil. Both claimed their way was the answer to life's purpose and meaning. Katie wished she knew which side possessed the truth. Sweet peace among the Comanches and the whites would be a true miracle.

Midmorning found her restless and irritable. When Katie began to feel frustrated in dealing with Jacob, she decided to take a walk. A heaviness rested upon the fort, as though the air carried some dreadful news. It seemed quieter than usual,

71

not the normal hustle and bustle that resounded from corner to corner. As Katie moved about the various activities, she noticed more soldiers posted in strategic points. Her eyes traveled upward to the canyon walls, and she searched for signs of Indians. Nothing moved out of the ordinary, but her heart pounded like war drums.

Katie looked out into the scenic beauty surrounding the fort. She pictured the ten-mile stretch known as Wild Rose Pass that rose from Black Mountain and looked down upon the fort. The pass was breathtaking, a welcome sight for any traveler who had weathered the desolate trail and warring Indians. The waters at the foot of the pass provided fresh fish, and Seth had taken Jacob there fishing on more than one occasion.

She observed a band of soldiers and civilians with oxen pulling a load of logs toward the fort. The armed men selected oak, pine, and cherry from the higher slopes to construct additional buildings within the stronghold. Katie wished they were the overdue patrol.

"What have your Comanche friends done with our soldiers?" a portly lady called out to her.

Katie recognized the woman, Mrs. Ames, an outspoken member of the church. She'd never heard a kind word from the woman and doubted if she ever would. Katie chose not to look her way; it would open her to more criticism and accusation. Instead she decided to walk back home and tend the garden for Elizabeth.

I wish I believed in God so I could pray for Peyton and the others, she thought. *At least I would feel like I was doing my part in the waiting.* Katie sighed deeply and fought the familiar lump rising in her throat. *Oh God, if You are there, would You please bring the soldiers back safely? I don't know what else to say or do, but ask if it is possible. Uncle Seth tells me that all things are possible with God, and he and Aunt Elizabeth along with lots of other folks are praying for them, too. I know I've asked for a sign, but it's more important for the men to be protected.*

Katie felt better, except she didn't know why.

Shortly after dusk while Seth, Elizabeth, and Katie quietly went about the evening chores, someone pounded on the door. Seth rose to receive the caller with Jacob trailing after him. Katie heard the sound of a man's voice.

"Peyton," Katie whispered. "Peyton!" She rushed to the door and nearly flung her arms around his neck but caught herself. "We were so worried about you," was all she could manage for tears stung her eyes and strangled any more words.

"I think you're glad to see me," Peyton grinned.

"Are the others unharmed?" Seth asked, ushering him inside.

"Yes, sir, God rode with us every step of the way and back."

"If you don't mind me asking, what delayed you?" Seth asked. "Folks were mighty worried."

"One of the men got a stomach ailment, and it passed around to all of us. We weren't able to complete our orders, and by the time we all recovered, our supplies were nearly gone."

Jacob moved shyly toward Peyton, and the sergeant chuckled. "Have I been gone that long, little man? I did take a bath before I came over, so I shouldn't be offensive." He bent down to Jacob's side and gave him a hug.

"Emily is walking," Jacob said proudly. "Here Emily." He motioned sweetly to his sister. "Walk over here to Sergeant Sinclair."

Elizabeth stood the child on the floor, and she walked toward her brother's outstretched hand. Everyone clapped and cheered as she fell into Peyton's arms. Katie felt a pang of regret that she, too, couldn't have reached out in affection toward the sergeant.

"Why don't you and Katie visit outside?" Seth suggested. "It will give you two some time alone. Katie has been ornery as a she-bear ever since you've been gone."

Katie denied any such actions and followed Peyton into the evening air. "I am so glad you are safe," she said once the door closed.

"I could tell," Peyton said with a quick laugh. "For a moment I thought I was going to get Katie Colter into my arms."

Katie felt herself grow warm, and she realized the telltale red had spread from her neck to her face. Immediately, she was thankful for the darkness concealing her embarrassment.

Within a few feet of the cabin, Peyton gathered her into his arms. "I've been wanting to do this for a long time," he said hoarsely.

Katie trembled uncontrollably. She willed it to stop, except the shaking continued. Peyton released her as though he had embraced a hot potato from a cooking pot.

"I'm sorry," he said. "I didn't mean to frighten you."

Katie licked dry lips; still she trembled. "I don't know why I am reacting like this," she said honestly. "I was so worried, and I missed you the first morning you were gone." Hesitantly, she touched the cuff of his sleeve.

"But you don't want me to hold you?" he asked. Peyton's question sounded kind, but she could tell he was hurt.

"Peyton, I'm not sure of what I want or need. So many things are going on in my head, and I wouldn't want you to think my feelings weren't honest."

"I understand," he said quietly. "I understand more than you may realize."

Katie relaxed slightly. Even though she knew Peyton had no idea what troubled her, his gentle words made her feel better.

"Can we walk a bit?" Katie asked. "Or are you too tired?"

"No, I'm just fine."

"Would you tell me what happened while you were gone?" she asked in order to change the way of their conversation.

"It's most likely boring—vomiting soldiers doesn't say much about heroic feats of valor."

"You have a point, a good one I might add. But I just

wondered if you met up with any Comanches."

"No. . .no problems at all. Like I said, nothing to report, only heat and empty prairie lands."

"Nothing seen or heard outside of these gates is boring— the land is beautiful and free."

"We did ride past your ranch," Peyton informed her. "Everything looked fine."

"Then you were in the heart of dangerous country," Katie commented. She paused, then added, "I asked God to keep you safe."

"And when did you pray for me?" Peyton asked.

Katie considered the time. "Yesterday, about midmorning, I was out walking, trying to rid myself of a sour mood."

"Oh, missing me put you in a sour mood?" Peyton asked teasingly. His tone quickly changed to a serious note. "Katie, did you say midmorning?"

"Yes, why?"

"God truly did watch over us," he whispered. "We were riding along the Teyah River when a peculiar feeling came over me. It was more of an urgency to turn the men around and ride out of there—fast. At the time, I felt foolish in giving the order, except now I believe the message came from God."

Katie stood speechless. She knew the area all too well. Comanches could have easily led them into an ambush. God did answer her prayer! And He gave her a sign, too! She must tell Uncle Seth; she must tell him that God answered her prayer.

"Katie, you are strangely quiet, more quiet than usual," Peyton said.

"I was thinking how God answered my prayer as soon as I spoke it. I've never confessed to believing in Him, and I prayed for you and the other soldiers out of desperation." Katie paused in her words before continuing. "I also asked God for a sign so I would know if He was real. . . . . He gave me both."

"Your aunt and uncle will be pleased," Peyton noted. "I've

been praying for you to find God, too."

"You have?" she asked incredulously. "Then I need to thank you."

"A hug would be nice, but I'll wait until you are ready. I need to get you back home before Colonel Ross sends someone to fetch me."

"Yes, of course, and I must tell Uncle Seth and Aunt Elizabeth everything," Katie said excitedly.

"You, tell everything and not keep a bit of it to yourself?" Peyton laughed. "Now God would be performing a miracle."

Back at the cabin, Peyton excused himself with the promise of visiting the next day. When Katie told Seth and Elizabeth about her prayer and Peyton's report of the incident along the Teyah River, Elizabeth cried and Seth hugged her. The three prayed together, and Seth led Katie to Christ.

Katie felt the tension of the past days vanish at the close of the prayer. Without being able to fully express her peace and joy, she opened the family Bible and found Psalm 40, where someone had clearly underlined the passage: "I waited patiently for the Lord; and he inclined unto me, and heard my cry. He brought me up also out of an horrible pit, out of the miry clay, and set my feet upon a rock and established my goings. And he hath put a new song in my mouth, even praise unto our God: many shall see it, and fear, and shall trust in the Lord. Blessed is that man that maketh the Lord his trust, and respecteth not the proud, nor such as turn aside to lies. Many, O Lord my God, are thy wonderful works which thou hast done, and thy thoughts which are to usward: they cannot be reckoned up in order unto thee: if I would declare and speak of them, they are more than can be numbered."

Katie knew the ache in her heart had been mended. Her new heavenly Father would direct her through the days ahead. She didn't expect things to be easy, only that God would be with her. And like Emily, Katie took the first steps into the arms of her heavenly Father.

nine

After Katie gave her heart to Jesus, she found a sense of peace and joy sprouting like wildflowers in spring. Seth said the Lord allowed gentleness and compassion to accompany Katie wherever she went. No longer did seriousness and sadness grace her lovely face, and she eagerly responded to helping others. Katie remembered a time when life produced little cares, but those days had now passed into an era of serving the Lord. Katie believed she must reach out to those who hurt. She wanted to soothe their pain, especially those who had endured tragic losses from the Comanches. The sensitive traits were real and a part of the child God created.

Seth told Katie that God put a special star in her eyes to light up the dark side of people. Every time she saw Emily toddle about on wobbly legs, it reminded her of holding onto God's hand while she stepped out in faith.

"Katie, child, do you plan to read the whole Bible tonight?" Seth asked one evening after she had read late into the night.

"Are you tired of my questions?" Katie teased.

"You haven't asked me any for the past hour," Seth said. "You must be preparing a hard one."

"No, Uncle Seth," she laughed. "I'm reading Psalms. Well, really I'm memorizing a few of the shorter ones."

"Good," Seth said. "Having God's Word stored in your heart is the best guard against Satan."

Elizabeth handed Katie a folded sheet of paper. "Here are the passages I promised you. The Scriptures listed here have brought me through many difficult times in my life. It's easy to turn to Psalms and praise God when life is good, but sometimes we need help when sorrow and grief seem to get the best of us."

"Thank you, Aunt Elizabeth," Katie said, looking over the paper. "I'll always treasure this."

"It was given to me a long time ago when I had fallen into self-pity about Seth and I not having any children. I took to memorizing each one of those passages. God is so faithful. The adoption proceedings for Jacob and Emily are moving along just fine, and we are so blessed to have been a part of your acceptance of God's grace."

"I can see these verses will give me strength when Peyton is on patrol. I know God is watching over the soldiers, but I still feel anxious about them. When the soldiers are here, the feelings disappear. Then Colonel Ross dispatches another group, and I worry again."

"Jeremiah 29 says: 'For I know the thoughts that I think toward you, saith the Lord, thoughts of peace, and not of evil, to give you an expected end. Then shall ye call upon Me, and ye shall go and pray unto Me, and I will harken unto you. And ye shall seek Me, and find Me, when ye shall seek Me with all your heart,'" Elizabeth quoted. "Those words have always gotten me through the roughest of days."

"We all tend to worry and fret over things we can't control," Seth said. "It's a part of our nature. Elizabeth tells me that you delivered a loaf of bread to Mrs. Ames. I am so proud of you."

Katie smiled. "She had become so critical and outspoken about Pa and our dealings with the Comanches that her disagreeable nature had almost become a game. Sometimes I guessed at what she would say next. You are the one who told me true obedience to God means doing those things that may not be pleasant. I've been trying to look at her through the eyes of Jesus, and it has helped." Katie laughed. "Uncle, Mrs. Ames didn't know what to say when I handed her the bread. She just took it and shut the door in my face."

"But you did your part," Seth reminded her. He reached down and planted a kiss on her forehead. "Goodnight, child. Don't read too late; you need your rest."

Katie read and reread those Biblical passages giving specific instructions about putting matters of concern into the hands of the Father. Even so, she still felt the apprehension. Katie hadn't seen or heard from the Kiowa, and she didn't know if his absence came as a curse or a blessing. Aunt Elizabeth said God warns His children about trying to solve their own problems instead of giving it all to Him. She said folks just don't seem to listen when God knows what is best for them.

☙

Martha added Jacob to her list of learners. When folks discovered Martha had once taught school, they asked to bring their own children. The parents paid Martha in food and chores while talk began of building a school. Katie habitually finished helping Elizabeth early enough to assist with the children's lessons. The hours Jeremiah had spent instructing Katie on how to read maps and live in the wild proved invaluable to Martha. The older woman used Katie's knowledge as a reward for the boys when they proved reluctant to study.

As Lauren's wedding day approached, Katie helped stitch linens and clothing to add to the bride's trousseau. The girls grew closer and shared their heartfelt dreams about their own future families. Martha accused the two of giggling more than they worked, but she also encouraged them to spend time together.

Peyton visited the Colter cabin nearly every day. Katie never knew when he would come calling; some days he arrived just before the children woke from their naps, and other days he came by in the evening. He always apologized for stopping by unannounced, and his visits were brief. Katie believed the short stays were due to her response toward his embrace. She wondered if Peyton thought his touch was repugnant when in fact she struggled with tender emotions. His presence brought on a whole new set of feelings for Katie, and it perplexed her more than she cared to admit. One thing she knew for certain: Peyton Sinclair was a good man, and she valued his friendship.

"Do you have a moment to talk?" Peyton asked one afternoon while the children slept.

Katie smiled warmly. "Of course I do."

"I wanted to thank you for telling me about your childhood with the Comanches," Peyton said. "As a soldier, I tend to forget the Indians love and care for their families. It didn't occur to me that they participate in games and enjoy life much like we do. You gave me a whole new perspective on why they hate the white man. We are a threat to everything they hold sacred."

Katie nodded reflectively. "I do have good memories, especially of Desert Fawn and how she took care of me after my mother died. I do regret that the Comanches do not know the one true God. If they did, perhaps we all could live in peace."

"Sounds like a child's story," Peyton said soberly.

"Yes, I guess it is."

"Were you given an Indian name?"

"Yes," Katie said, recalling the first time Jeremiah whispered it in her ear. "Swift Arrow gave it to me after he and my father became friends. I suppose you want to know what it is."

"Of course."

"Yo-oh-hobt Paph. It means yellow hair."

"It suits you," Peyton said with a wide grin. "Did your father call you this openly?"

"Most of the time. He called me Katie when we were alone and especially near the end." She felt uneasy with the topic of conversation focusing on her.

"I have a new curiosity about the Comanche," Peyton stated.

Katie heard Emily start to stir, and she lifted the toddler into her arms.

"And what is your question?" Katie asked. "I might not be

able to answer it."

"I thought you were the expert," he stated in pretended shock. "I'm sure you won't disappoint me. Now, I've heard that Comanche war bonnets were made entirely of eagle feathers."

"You heard correctly. Other tribes dye turkey feathers for their war bonnets, but to a Comanche that would be a disgrace."

"See, you did know the answer," Peyton said. "And I thank you."

"The Comanches are a proud race," Katie said thoughtfully. "They won't be driven from this land without a fight."

"Excuse me if this offends you, but Katie, do you miss them?" Peyton asked. He studied her face intently.

Katie considered his question and realized he did not intend to insult her. "Sometimes I think about the people I grew to love, but my home is here. I'm happy and I belong to the family of God. What more could I want?"

Peyton reached to take Emily from Katie's arms. "Sounds to me like you have everything you need," Peyton commented oddly.

Katie's eyes flew to his face. What was that she saw?

❧

Katie carried a basket of cornbread, roast duck, and apple pie to Martha's family. Most of the children had been down with colds and fever, and the food would be welcomed for the evening meal.

As usual when Peyton rode patrol, Katie's thoughts turned to the increasing number of Comanche raids. The news inevitably devastated her as much as the families of the injured or killed. The horrible injustices done to innocent families and the thought of old familiar faces seeking out white settlers made her feel responsible. In one breath she realized the incidents were not her fault, and in the next breath guilt washed over every part of her. Katie worried and fretted until Peyton rode through the front gate. Many times she wondered why he had to lead every group of soldiers who checked on Indian activity, but by the time she saw him again, the question slipped her mind.

Katie continued on her walk, but as she passed the colonel's office, she spied a shiny rock near the side of the small building. Katie smiled and stepped closer. It would certainly gain Jacob's attention. She stooped to pick it up and heard voices.

"Two more families were found murdered and their homes burned to the ground," one soldier reported. "Besides being scalped, the whole family, even the children, were tortured before they died."

Katie shuddered. Peyton never shared the grotesque details about his encounters with raiding Indians. She felt grateful to him for shielding her from the truth.

"Pardon me, sir, but we need to wipe out the whole Indian nation—women and children, too. I'm for burning their villages to the ground. Let them get a dose of their own medicine," another soldier stated.

The colonel cleared his throat. "It's the land. The Indians believe we have no right to be here, and they are going to do their best to drive us out. Our job is to stop the raids so folks can live on their land without fear of losing their hair. Sooner or later those savages will realize that there are a lot more of us than them."

When will this ever end? Katie asked herself. *Can't God soften the soldiers' and the Indians' hearts to stop this senseless killing? Why can't both sides simply talk and work out a peaceable solution?* Katie remembered her father had traded furs, food, and horses for their ranch. It seemed fair to her.

"Lone Eagle appears to be leading more raids than his father. Reminds me of a rattler—ready to strike when you least expect it," the colonel said. "I wonder if he's human, and I'd like the honor of blowing a hole right through his chest."

With Colonel Ross's statement, Katie realized her feelings

for the warrior had been laid to rest. She feared Lone Eagle just like those around her. Perhaps Lone Eagle had merely been a young girl's infatuation, but now nothing remained but best forgotten memories. His actions churned her stomach.

"When is Sergeant Sinclair due back?" the first soldier asked again.

"Yesterday," the colonel replied. "He's a good soldier, and I would hate to lose him. I want to know the moment he returns."

Katie had heard enough. She hurried around to the front of the colonel's office and walked briskly toward the Jamesons' cabin. Her heart lifted a prayer for Peyton's safe return and an end to the bloodshed.

On the way back from her errand, Katie heard a commotion at the front gate. Peyton and his patrol had returned safely. He waved, and she felt her heart soar.

❄

The day of Lauren's wedding came, and Katie felt as excited as the young bride. Katie had sewn, baked, and assisted in the events leading up to the day ever since she met Lauren. The groom's name was Miles Barrett—a comely man who had earned the reputation as an excellent soldier and was well respected among the civilians. He accompanied Peyton on most of the patrols, and Peyton had remarked more than once on his clear thinking in the line of duty.

Lauren and Miles were clearly devoted to each other, and both of them had dedicated their lives to the Lord. For Katie, this marriage stated one more reason why the Comanche dispute needed to be resolved. Lauren shouldn't be afraid when Miles rode out on patrol.

Except for the soldiers guarding the fort, most everyone planned to attend the wedding ceremony. When Reverend Cooper saw the number of folks gathered to seat themselves inside his small hutlike church, he immediately moved the wedding outside. Roughly constructed benches were snatched up like kindling and arranged in the open air. When the benches could fit no more guests, families stood together noisily waiting for the bride to make her appearance.

Katie felt enthralled with the excitement brewing in the air. Standing with Seth and Elizabeth, she realized she didn't ever want to return to the Indians. Here dwelled her family and her God.

Lauren and Miles's wedding served to remind Katie of how close she came to spending the rest of her life with a Comanche warrior. She searched the crowd for the Kiowa, all the while the old gnawing fear crept over her again.

"Are you looking for someone?" Elizabeth asked.

Relieved that the Indian was not among them, Katie pushed away any thoughts of Lone Eagle demanding she return to him.

"I just wondered about one of the soldiers, but he's not here," Katie said. If Lone Eagle truly meant to threaten her into obedience, the Kiowa would have long since found a way to tell her. "This is simply wonderful," she said, breathless with the excitement.

She turned her attention to the bride walking slowly past her. Lauren's father held his daughter's arm while she steadied a Bible with her other hand. Martha and Elizabeth had searched frantically for a bouquet of wildflowers to arrange into a bouquet, but Lauren insisted upon carrying her Bible with several satin ribbons instead.

"Isn't she beautiful?" Elizabeth murmured as Lauren brushed by them.

Katie could only nod. She felt her eyes moisten with joy for her dear friend.

"Look at her dress, Katie. I'd never seen it on her before," Elizabeth sighed. "Martha said it was her grandmother's wedding dress. Mercy me, it hugs her waist just right. I declare she looks more like a precious china doll than a prairie bride."

The dress's color had faded to ivory along with the many

yards of delicate lace, yet the shade of the wedding gown enhanced Lauren's clay-colored hair and sky blue eyes. Pearl buttons lined a high, lace-trimmed neck and lay within the scallops of the neck, sleeves, bodice, and layered skirt.

Katie listened to the parting crowd whisper "ooh" and "ah" as the bride fairly floated past them. Lauren's face glowed, and her eyes sparkled. Katie believed Lauren was the most beautiful bride in the world.

As radiant as the bride appeared, the groom looked every bit as dashing. Every metal accessory on his uniform glistened. "Looks to me like folks could see themselves in Miles's boots," Seth chuckled. "And he must have been up all night polishing the buttons on his uniform."

All the people who sat or stood near the young couple detected a slight trembling in the groom, especially as Lauren moved closer to him.

Katie caught a glimpse of Peyton as he took his place beside Miles as the best man. He took her breath away. Katie wondered if she would ever marry a man as fine as Sergeant Peyton Sinclair.

"Dearly beloved," the preacher began.

With all of the planning of the past several weeks, the wedding ceremony ended all too quickly. Reverend Cooper delivered a short sermon on the biblical principles of a sound marriage, and Lauren and Miles whispered their vows. The crowd hushed to see them seal their promises with a kiss.

"And now I would like to introduce you to the new Mr. and Mrs. Miles Barrett. Lauren and Miles, you may greet your friends and family," Reverend Cooper announced.

Katie heard the soldiers cheer and other folks clap their hands. A chain of laughter echoed across the fort and over the canyon walls. The merriment would now begin.

"Join us for food and fellowship," Mr. Jameson shouted, and pointed in the direction of the cabin where everyone was to gather.

"I've got my fiddle," a soldier shouted.

Elizabeth, Katie, and Martha, plus three of Lauren's sisters assembled around two makeshift tables outside of the Jameson home. One table held all sorts of canned fruits, vegetables, preserves, delicate needlepoint items, tools, and even dry goods for the new couple to set up housekeeping. The second table held cake, pies, and fruit cobblers with a huge bowl of punch. The desserts were placed on several donated sets of dishes and even more sets of cups. Elizabeth and Martha served the food while Katie alternated with Lauren's sisters in pouring punch and washing dirty dishes.

At first all of them busied themselves in helping folks get food and drink, but when the line of guests dwindled, the servers relaxed and treated themselves. No sooner had Katie sliced herself a piece of apple pie than Peyton appeared.

"Have you eaten?" Katie asked.

"Yes, ma'am," Peyton replied. "You were inside the cabin when I went through the line."

"Good, because I'm starved."

"I think it's traditional for those who serve not to eat the food," Peyton said casually. "It's a custom that is strictly enforced."

Katie glanced up, eyes open wide, embarrassed at the thought of breaking a social rule.

"Especially apple pie—that's always for the best man," Peyton said.

"And you're teasing me," Katie pointed out. "I don't know how you can tell such tales with a straight face."

"Years of practice," Peyton said, but he grinned widely. "Can you get away for a little while?"

Katie looked around and saw nothing for her to do.

"Aunt Elizabeth, will things here be all right for a while?" she asked.

"Certainly, you've done plenty for one day," Elizabeth replied.

Katie and Peyton left the crowd of people behind and made their way through the front gate to the beauty of Limpia Valley. They talked of the wedding, the cooler weather, and Emily and Jacob's latest accomplishments. Jacob loved learning, and he'd already learned his letters. Emily spoke new words almost on a daily basis. Both she and Jacob called Elizabeth and Seth Mama and Papa.

Peyton pointed in the direction of Black Mountain, the tallest of its kind, and the beautiful Wild Rose Pass.

"See up there," Peyton pointed to Black Mountain. "When I see the beauty of that canyon pass, then I know I'm nearly home."

"I wish you could send me a signal, so then I could stop praying and fretting about you," Katie said.

"Did you know that you are the first person I rush to see after I've reported to the colonel?" Peyton asked. "Of course I clean up first, or you would smell me coming." They had stopped to admire nature's sculpture and enjoy the unseasonably warm fall temperatures.

"I wasn't aware of such things," Katie replied, pretending to be unimpressed. "But thank you, especially for the bath."

A slight breeze met their faces, and the two quietly enjoyed the refreshing touch of fall. Soon winter, with all of its whistling winds and freezing temperatures, would keep them huddled around a warm fire.

Peyton took Katie's hand and together they strolled by the stream that fed Limpia Valley. "After being a part of Miles and Lauren's wedding I now wonder how Comanches marry."

"It's quite different," Katie said. "Comanche couples are not supposed to ever talk, but they usually devise ways to meet in secret. If a warrior has serious intentions, then he simply presents the maiden's family with gifts, usually horses. If the parents accept the gifts, then the couple begins living together and they are considered married. Sometimes the warrior will try to sneak into the bride's tent to snatch her away. Providing he's successful, then he has a wife."

"I think their way sounds better than ours," Peyton said, obviously amused. "Except you must have a lot of horses to win your lady's hand. What if the girl doesn't want to marry the warrior?"

"She can urge her parents not to accept the gifts; but if her parents approve, she's stuck with her husband."

"I change my mind," Peyton said. "I like the idea of courtin' a girl instead of buying off her parents."

Katie laughed and he squeezed her hand.

"You're on my mind most all of the time," Peyton said seriously. He faced her squarely, and his endearing look caused her heart to pound furiously. She didn't tremble like before, but silently captured her own feelings and admitted to herself much more than a mere attraction to Peyton.

"I would like to pull you close to me," Peyton said softly. "Except the last time I frightened you."

Katie turned away, then bravely met his ardent gaze with her own shy longings. "I won't stop you this time," she said.

Peyton reached to hold her close, and she felt his breath brush against her cheek. She hoped he didn't hear the rapid beating of her heart, for she felt certain it would give away the secrets she needed to safeguard.

"We need to talk," Peyton said hoarsely, winding his fingers through her hair. "There are things, important things I must tell you." He gingerly released her and stepped back to study the young woman before him. "Katie, I care for you very much—more than caring, I love you."

Katie opened her mouth to speak, but his fingers silenced any response.

"Wait, let me finish, because I may not have the courage to tell you this again. I realized I loved you the night we learned about Jacob and Emily's family. Any other woman would have steered clear from such a nightmare, but you bravely insisted upon coming with me. When I saw the look of compassion upon your face at the sight of Jacob holding his little sister, I knew God had set you apart from all other women for me." Peyton paused before beginning again. "Even though you didn't have Jesus in your life, a lot of folks, besides myself, were praying for you. And when you did accept Him, I realized God *had* put you into my life for a purpose."

"But there are things you don't know about me," Katie softly protested.

"I know enough to see God's purpose in the both of us together," Peyton said. "And I, too, have things to tell you—some of which I regret, but they must be told." Peyton gently grasped both of Katie's hands and held her at arm's length from him. "I'm not proud of what the army has always asked of me, Katie, and one of the areas of duty has caused me to deceive you."

Katie could only stare at him in wonder. Had Peyton led patrols of men to destroy old men, women, and children living in Indian villages? Had Lone Eagle been killed? Peyton did not know of her relationship with the Comanche warrior, unless Uncle Seth had told him. Had Peyton been transferred to another post and was now hesitant to tell her? Peyton's face appeared pained, and Katie could not imagine what could possibly disturb him so greatly.

"Peyton, my feelings for you are new, and despite my awkwardness in all of this, I want you to understand you can tell me anything. . .because Jesus loves me and forgives me. . . and because I care for you very much. I've fought any type of emotion for you, and I can't believe I am admitting it to you now. What I am trying to say is it sounds like we both have things from our past to tell the other, but it shouldn't change how we feel." Katie wiped the tears slipping down over her face and realized she trembled. She stepped into his embrace, and he wrapped his arms around her. "Peyton, I feel so guilty and ashamed about living with the Comanches. Uncle Seth and Aunt Elizabeth say I shouldn't, but every time I see someone who has been hurt by them, I despise myself."

"Sweetheart, God knows your heart. How can you blame yourself for their actions? You were a child living with those who treated you with love and kindness."

"And I loved them."

"Is not love the greatest commandment? Don't ever regret the time you spent with those people. You learned how they think and what they feel. Too bad the rest of us can't do the same thing. Maybe then we would have peace. Katie, listen to me for one moment. I have not been truthful with you. . ."

A shout from the distance alerted Peyton. A young boy rode in their direction. The couple watched the rider approach and recognized Lauren's brother.

"Miss Colter, you're needed at the reception," he said breathlessly. "Lauren is ready to toss her ribbons to the next bride, and she won't budge an inch until you get there."

ten

Katie caught Lauren's ribbons. She blushed and denied any truth in an upcoming wedding with Sergeant Sinclair, but Peyton only grinned and refused to comment. As the wedding celebration continued until after dusk, Peyton and Katie didn't find an opportunity to speak further. Once they attempted to leave the festivities for a few moments, except Miles spied them and urged them to stay awhile longer.

Evening shadows forced everyone to their homes, and Peyton reluctantly informed Katie of a patrol scheduled to ride out before sunup. The soldiers would be gone for three weeks, escorting several wagons carrying provisions and supplies through Comanche territory.

"Don't you go getting into a sour mood," Peyton teasingly said. It had become his favorite parting remark, and the words always made her smile.

He walked her to the cabin door; both were reluctant to say goodnight. "I will do my best to stay sweet," Katie assured him.

Peyton said goodnight and started to walk away, but he abruptly turned to face her. "Katie, I have never kissed you; I've certainly thought about it enough. Every time I'm ready, something or somebody interrupts us."

"There's nothing stopping you now," she said softly. "Unless you don't want to."

"Oh, I want to. Guess I'd better take advantage of the dark while I can," Peyton said.

Katie thought her heart would burst through her chest; surely Peyton could hear it flutter as his lips descended upon hers so slowly and gently, as though he wanted the kiss to last forever. He took her face into his hands and brushed a kiss to her forehead, the peak of her nose, and lightly against her lips.

"I love you, Katie Colter," Peyton whispered in her ear, and then he was gone.

Late into the night Katie's mind lingered on the events of the day. What a perfect day for a wedding, and she felt so happy for Lauren and Miles. She remembered suddenly that Peyton had wanted to tell her about a matter of importance. It had seemed urgent, and for a moment Katie wondered what it could be. Peyton stood for all God rendered as right and good.

Katie didn't intend to cry with his departure, but alone on her mat she muffled the tears. She had been ready to tell Peyton about Lone Eagle and the Kiowa scout. Her tears fell in fear for his safety. And she realized she should have told him about her relationship with the warrior. Now she must wait to uncover the ugly truth about herself.

❧

As before, Katie threw herself into any work or activity that would keep her mind occupied until the patrol returned. She comforted herself by memorizing psalms, allowing their words to flow through her until she felt the blessings of praising God. Many times she daydreamed of Peyton and his endearing words of love. Katie prayed for God's guidance and direction with Peyton; she felt certain God wanted them together.

"Katie, child, you certainly have been smiling a lot here lately," Elizabeth remarked as they tidied the cabin. "Does the sergeant have anything to do with this?"

"Well, I don't know," Katie said, trying to appear surprised at her aunt's statement.

"Yes, you do," Elizabeth said, attempting to conceal a laugh. "You have the glow of a lady in love."

"Do I?" Katie asked, then laughed in spite of her resolve to appear coy.

"So, tell your dear aunt what happened the day of Lauren and Miles's wedding," Elizabeth coaxed. "You have been radiant ever since."

"You don't think it's because I'm happy for Lauren?" Katie asked, picking up a corn husk broom to sweep the rough stone floor.

"No, miss. So you might as well tell me—I won't stop pestering you until you do," Elizabeth stated with one hand on her hip and pointing her finger with the other.

Katie wondered if she should tell Elizabeth; she hadn't told a soul about her and Peyton's conversation. Suddenly Katie smiled broadly. "Well. . .it's very good. . . . He told me he cared for me, and I told him I felt the same."

"Something tells me those weren't the exact words," Elizabeth said.

"Probably not, but they are pretty close," Katie said, still laughing. "Honestly, Aunt Elizabeth, both of us feel God has put us together, and we are very happy."

"Any mention of marriage?"

"Not the word 'marriage,' but a hint of it," Katie said shyly, then she lifted her chin stubbornly. "And that's all I can say until Peyton gets back and we have time to talk."

"I'm so happy for you," Elizabeth said with tears in her eyes. She shook her head as if to ignore the drops falling down her cheeks.

"I still have to tell him about Lone Eagle," Katie said soberly. "And I will as soon as he gets back."

"Yes, it's best to be honest about everything with those you love," Elizabeth said. "Seth and I started our marriage with that belief, and I believe its sound advice for all couples."

Admitting out loud her love for Peyton made it real. The words spilled out like a bubbling waterfall, and she didn't care who could see or hear it. The patrol couldn't arrive home any too soon.

&

Three weeks turned into four and still no word from the supply train or the army patrol. Katie gave the soldiers three more days' grace to allow for broken wheels or any other reasons why they would be delayed. On the morning of the fourth day, she chose to go see the colonel herself. After all, Colonel Ross should know why they were late, and he might answer her questions.

Katie nervously knocked on the officer's door. When she didn't hear a reply, she knocked again a little harder. Each time her knuckles rapped against the wooden door, her impatience mounted.

"I said, come in," the colonel bellowed behind the door.

Katie stepped inside and noted Colonel Ross hadn't reduced the stack of papers on his desk from the last time she was there. In fact, the mound of documents looked larger. He glanced up and surprise etched the lines around his eyes.

"Miss Colter, excuse me. I didn't expect it to be you. Do sit down."

Katie obediently seated herself on the ladder-back chair in front of the desk. "I won't take much of your time, Colonel Ross. I just have a few questions," Katie began. She took a deep breath and willed her voice to stop shaking.

"You can have all of the time you need. Is it about your land? If so, I haven't gotten the paperwork back from the territorial land office." He leaned back in his chair and eyed her curiously.

"It's not about the land," Katie said.

"I didn't think so; you look too upset."

"The patrol is very late," Katie said as slowly and precisely as possible. "I was wondering if you had heard any word from them."

The colonel sighed deeply and picked up his pipe. "No, I haven't, but as soon as I do, I will be happy to inform you of their status." His manner was so formal that Katie wondered how many others had requested the same information.

"I realize you are busy, I'm just concerned," she said apologetically.

"Your interest is understandable. Any number of reasons could delay them."

Katie rose to leave. "Thank you, sir, for your time. I will

continue to pray for their safe return."

"I'm sure the men appreciate your prayers, Miss Colter."

"Colonel?" Katie asked with a degree of hesitancy. She latched on to the back of the wooden chair as though it would support her impending question.

"Yes."

"Why does Sergeant Sinclair accompany every one of the patrols?"

"Well, that's simple," the colonel said. "He's the only enlisted man who speaks Comanche."

Katie's face paled. She fought a sick feeling in the bottom of her stomach, and the room seemed to spin. It couldn't be true, but she'd heard Colonel Ross state so: Peyton spoke Comanche. No wonder he rode with every soldier who rode in and out of Fort Davis. His skills were vital in conversing, even surviving, with the Indians. Obviously the Kiowa scout didn't know Peyton spoke Comanche, or he wouldn't have spoken with her.

"Why wasn't I told this the afternoon Peyton escorted me to your office? Surely you remember when the Kiowa asked to speak with me?" Katie realized her voice sounded distant as though someone else spoke through her lips.

"I didn't feel it necessary," the colonel began.

"You didn't feel it necessary," Katie felt her voice rising. "Did you think I might reveal some valuable information you could use against the Comanches?"

"I believe you misunderstood. . ."

Katie interrupted the colonel's explanation. "I do understand, Colonel Ross. You wanted to make sure I wasn't some kind of a spy. Goodness, Jeremiah Colter's daughter must have been sent here to get information for the Comanches. Was the Kiowa's request a trap? And is his absence from the fort a way to make the meeting look real? Thank you, Colonel, for the confidence. I'm sure your interpreter gave you a favorable report."

eleven

Katie didn't remember walking home after the meeting with Colonel Ross, neither did she recall anyone she passed. Her thoughts were fixed on the colonel's truth and the likelihood of Peyton befriending her for the army's use. She didn't want to believe he would deliberately use her affections to gather information for the army, but the colonel's words made it appear so. Blinding, stinging tears humiliated her, and anger burned like a raging prairie fire.

At home Elizabeth tried to get her to explain what happened, but Katie simply paced the floor and shed tear after tear. Finally she picked up Emily and attempted to rock her. When holding the toddler didn't bring comfort, she held Emily close and wept more. Jacob patted her on the shoulder and whispered, "It will be all right," much like she had done with him.

"Has something happened to Peyton?" Elizabeth asked, kneeling beside the rocking chair.

Katie shook her head no.

"I can't help you if you don't tell me what is wrong," Elizabeth said softly. She pulled a wet strand of hair from Katie's face and tucked it behind her ear.

Katie took a deep breath. "I just found out that Colonel Ross and Peyton arranged a meeting with a Kiowa scout to see if I would send information back to. . ." Katie couldn't finish with Jacob standing so near.

"Surely not," Elizabeth said indignantly. "It has to be a mistake."

"The colonel just told me," Katie said between sobs. She carefully retold the accounting, making sure to leave out certain words that would alarm Jacob.

"There has to be a reasonable explanation, surely a misunderstanding," Elizabeth said. "But right now, you need to get alone with the Lord. You will be miserable until you pray and find the courage to forgive both of them."

"Forgive them?" Katie asked quickly. "How can I ever forgive or forget?"

"Not on your own strength, but with the power of God," her aunt responded. Elizabeth picked up a brown package and placed it in Katie's lap. "Here, we've been saving this for you. It's a new Bible, a gift from your uncle and me. We planned to give it to you this evening, but you have greater use for it now."

Elizabeth lifted Emily from Katie's lap and watched while her niece untied the heavy string around the package. Katie drew a brown leather Bible to her chest and mouthed a tearful thank you.

"Go on into our room," Elizabeth urged. "Spend time alone with the Father. Only He can comfort you."

Katie seldom entered her aunt and uncle's bedroom. She and the children slept in the main part of the two-room cabin and found no need to step inside Seth and Elizabeth's small bit of privacy.

Sitting in a wooden chair on which a quilt had been draped over the back, Katie wiped the tears from her eyes and silently prayed before opening the Bible.

Oh, heavenly Father, I hurt so badly. I feel like my whole world has just fallen down around me. I don't know why Peyton didn't tell me he spoke Comanche, and I don't know why he couldn't trust me enough to tell me he understood the Kiowa's words. I feel so horrible, and the ache in my heart is worse than when Pa died. At least he didn't have a choice, but Peyton chose to deceive me.

Katie stopped in the middle of her prayer. Peyton had used the word "deceive" when he tried to tell her something before he left on patrol. It had to be this, nothing else would have affected him with such urgency. Opening the Bible, she prayed for God to speak to her through His Word.

The dedication page was empty, and Katie decided to ask Seth and Elizabeth to complete it. If they had gone ahead with their plans to present the Bible to her that evening, the blank lines would have been filled.

Leafing through page after page, Katie read passages that comforted her but none that pierced her heart. Then 1 Corinthians, chapter 13 caught her eye. Katie read it once and wept in the knowledge of God's love for her and His infinite understanding of her feelings. She reread the description of love, blinking back the tears and thanking God for His Word. Verse 8 spoke directly to the pain in her heart. "Charity never faileth: but whether there be prophecies, they shall fail; whether there be tongues, they shall cease; whether there be knowledge, it shall vanish away." And on to verse 13: "For now we see through a glass darkly; but then face to face: now I know in part, but then shall I know even as also I am known. And now abideth faith, hope, and charity, these three; but the greatest of these is charity."

Katie closed the book and let it rest upon her lap. What Colonel Ross and Peyton did was wrong. They had deceived her in order to see if she would willingly side with the Comanches. Katie also wondered if the colonel and Peyton contrived the Kiowa's questioning. She quickly dispelled the latter thought; the Kiowa spoke of matters known only by Lone Eagle and herself.

Katie sat upright as she realized Peyton knew of her relationship with Lone Eagle. He had heard the Kiowa issue Lone Eagle's demands, and he clearly heard her answers. Peyton had known all along and never said a word. It was as though it didn't matter to him. *That's why he was so angry that day,* she thought. The guilt she bore for not telling him about the warrior didn't seem to matter now. Yet, beyond any measure of doubt, Peyton clearly understood her loyalties. Katie had feared rejection from Peyton when he learned the truth, and he had already heard the truth from her own lips.

Now she saw why the Kiowa had been released from his duties at the fort. The Indian could not be trusted. If Peyton did use her, why did he later pursue a relationship?

How much of the conversation did Peyton reveal to the colonel? Katie felt so humiliated that the commander of the post might know intimate information about her. Perhaps Peyton kept some of the knowledge to himself. In any event, Katie must forgive them for purposely misleading her. And no matter the outcome, Katie must ask Peyton to forgive her for not telling him about Lone Eagle from the very beginning.

Katie closed her eyes and prayed for guidance. She leaned back against the quilt and slept.

She woke to the sound of Elizabeth's voice calling her to waken.

"Yes," Katie responded. "I fell asleep, Aunt Elizabeth. I'm sorry."

Elizabeth pushed aside the blanket separating the two rooms of the cabin. "Katie, Peyton is here with the colonel. They are waiting to see you."

The news cleared any sleepiness lingering in Katie's mind. "They both are here to see me," she whispered.

"Yes, child. I invited them in, but they decided to wait outside."

Katie stood and laid her Bible on the bed. "I guess I'd better see what they want." Then she added, "Peyton is all right, isn't he?"

"He looks tired, but healthy," Elizabeth assured her. "I'm going to take the children to visit Seth."

"No, please. I can talk to them outside or go to the colonel's office," Katie insisted.

"You aren't the only Colter who is stubborn," informed Elizabeth. "And I've already told Jacob we would be leaving for the blacksmith."

Katie saw no use in arguing with her aunt. Elizabeth ushered the men inside to the table, poured them coffee, and left with the children to see Seth.

Katie avoided any eye contact with either one of them. She no longer felt like crying or shouting accusations. It seemed simpler to hear why the two had chosen to visit.

"Colonel Ross, I owe you an apology for my outburst in your office today," Katie said simply.

"Under the circumstances, I don't believe an apology is necessary," the colonel replied.

"There's no excuse for my rudeness, and I am sorry. Colonel Ross, Peyton, you didn't need to pay me a call." She turned to Peyton for the first time but still avoided his gaze. "I'm glad to see you returned safe and unharmed. Are the other men all right?"

Peyton sighed deeply. "Yes, just wore out."

The men sat stiffly at the table, but Katie chose the rocker near the fire. She wondered if she would ever feel comfortable with Colonel Ross or Peyton again.

"Miss Colter, Sergeant Sinclair and I are the ones who owe you an apology for what appears to be a misunderstanding or rather an oversight on our part. My reasons for accompanying the sergeant are to tell you myself that there was no pretense in the meeting you had with the Kiowa. The scout came into my office and stated he needed to speak with you. I sensed an importance in the matter and sent the sergeant to fetch you. In case you may have questioned my motives, I do not speak Comanche; therefore, I have no idea what transpired in your conversation. The sergeant told me you relayed perfectly the Kiowa's words, and I chose not to ask anything more about the subject but to take heed as you suggested. As I said to you after the Kiowa left my office, I appreciate your concern for the welfare of the people living here at Fort Davis. I chose to allow the Kiowa to come and go here to use his treachery against him, and I purposely provided him with false information."

The colonel stood from his chair. "I sincerely hope you will give this young man an opportunity to clear up this unfortunate incident."

Katie nodded and escorted him to the door. "Thank you for everything you just told me and for coming by to see me," she said. "I am sincerely grateful, and again I apologize for earlier today."

Once the door closed, Katie leaned against it. She felt Peyton's eyes bore through her, but she couldn't bring herself to face him.

"Am I so repulsive that you can't look at me?" Peyton asked, obviously exhausted and irritated.

Katie shook her head and noted the worried frown in his forehead. She forced herself to meet his gaze. "No, I really don't know what to say or do. I've been angry, I've been hurt, and now I'm confused and ashamed."

"Why are you ashamed?" he asked softly.

Katie took a deep breath. "Because I was busy feeling sorry for myself, and I forgot to consider the information you found out about me."

"Are you talking about your relationship with Lone Eagle?"

"Yes, and I am very sorry for not telling you about him the first night you asked to come calling," Katie said. She remained against the door as though it helped her from crumbling before his eyes.

"And I apologize for not telling you of my ability to speak Comanche," Peyton said. "I know it's no excuse, but I tried on several occasions."

"The afternoon of Lauren and Miles's wedding?" Katie asked as she moved away from the door and sat across from Peyton at the table. "Because I wanted to tell you about Lone Eagle then, too. I didn't want to keep it from you any longer."

Peyton shook his head as though he attempted to clear his thoughts. "I should have told you right from the start, and I did try the day of the wedding. Katie, if I learned anything the night you met with the Kiowa, it was how you were willing to go back with him to save the lives of people here. How could I be angry at your unselfish gesture?"

Katie looked down at her hands neatly folded in her lap. "I never looked at it quite the same way as you do. I kept remembering Jacob and Emily's family and wanted to see it ended. You see, I'm not afraid of Lone Eagle, and at one time I believed I loved him. I don't want to ever go back there, but if I had to, it wouldn't be a terrible sacrifice."

Peyton reached across the table and wrapped his hands over hers. His voice sounded raspy, and when Katie looked into his gray eyes, she saw emotion steal across his face. "Promise me you won't ever go back to him."

"I can't, Peyton," Katie said softly. "I can't promise you something that might endanger innocent lives. I love you; I love you with all my heart, but I couldn't live with myself if one person was injured or killed to ensure my happiness."

"Must you be so noble?" Peyton demanded.

Katie lifted her hand to his cheek. "I'm not noble, no, nothing of the sort. I'm trying to live my life as God would want, and I'll go wherever He leads me."

"Away from me, away from a life together?" he asked angrily.

"I pray it won't come to a choice," Katie said. She felt the tears fill her eyes. "I don't want to live my life with one man and love another."

twelve

Long, uncomfortable moments followed with the sounds of outside activity deafening the roar in Katie's heart. She wanted to tell Peyton the many things she dreamed for both of them and the countless hours spent watching the fort gate and praying for his safe return. The look on his face silenced any words of endearment; Katie remembered seeing the same expression on his face the night she refused to tell him what the Kiowa had relayed to her. They had quarreled then, and she didn't want to fall into the same pit again. Arguing solved nothing; it only deepened the problem.

Katie ordered herself to say nothing more in her own defense but allow Peyton to express his indignation. Except this time frustration and anger weren't the only emotions tearing through him; Katie saw a mixture of love and hate intertwined to add confusion to his passion. Dared she hope the hatred was not intended for her?

Dear Lord, I couldn't bear it if Peyton should hate me, but I can't make empty promises. My first love is You and the things You would desire of me.

She waited for Peyton to speak and for God to answer her prayer.

"The Kiowa should have tried to contact you by now," Peyton said bitterly. "He could have used any excuse to gain entrance into the fort."

"I agree," Katie said simply. "I look for him every day."

"Then marry me now, Katie. Marry me before Lone Eagle has a chance to use his power over you."

Katie shook her head and blinked back the tears. "Don't you see? It wouldn't change a thing but make matters worse.

103

In his eyes, I am his wife."

"It wasn't consummated," Peyton said hastily, and Katie wondered if he had memorized every word from the Kiowa's conversation.

"No, but my leaving him hurt his pride."

"I don't care about his pride! What kind of a man would want a woman who didn't want him?" Peyton asked. He pounded his fist into the table as though the physical action would make her agree with his words. Katie vowed not to lose her temper, and silence exploded from the four walls of the cabin.

Finally she spoke, but her voice cracked and shook. "But I grew up with Lone Eagle. I know him. He would use the lapse of time for his own benefit. Lone Eagle is known among the other warriors for his shrewd and cunning ways. Waiting is one of his favorite games. My fear is he will do nothing until he thinks I no longer believe he will send word. That's when Lone Eagle will make his declaration. Peyton, it's not an affair of the heart for him; it's a way of life, and he must win. No matter if he loved me beyond any doubt, Lone Eagle would still be a warrior. By waiting to speak until I have made other plans," Katie paused and felt herself grow warm with the implication of her words, "he causes me to fall into his trap, and then he will wage war and declare me a liar. Lone Eagle does not make idle threats or speak empty words, for that would discredit him in the eyes of his people."

"Remember when the Kiowa said Swift Arrow and Lone Eagle would not declare war over a woman but over honor and the land of their fathers?" Peyton reminded her.

Katie slowly nodded her head. "Yes, but I am his property, and in Lone Eagle's eyes his wife has run from him."

Peyton again pounded his fist into the wooden table. "I will see that murdering Indian burn in. . ."

"Peyton, calm down," Katie said hastily.

"And what would you have me do?" Peyton demanded.

"Sit back and allow Lone Eagle to decide your future, our future? I am a man, Katie, not a child who allows others to make his decisions for him."

"We could pray," Katie half pleaded. "We should turn this whole thing over to God and allow Him to work it out."

Peyton stood and walked to the door. "I can't pray right now. I'm too angry, and the thought of you allowing a murdering savage to determine our happiness is more than I can handle." He lifted the latch and closed the door soundly behind him.

Katie looked around the empty room. *What do I do now, God?* she asked.

Trust Me, Katie came a clear, quiet answer.

❧

Katie spent the remainder of the daylight hours contemplating what she should do about Peyton. She prayed for him and asked God to be with him, but little else could be done. Peyton needed to search for his own answers and allow God to work in his life. *I have to wait for Peyton to come to me,* she thought ironically. *Waiting. . .is what Lone Eagle does best, not me.*

She fully understood the Comanche warrior held her future, and she never doubted for a moment that the Kiowa had delivered her message. Lone Eagle deliberately chose not to send a reply. Katie felt he stalked his prey well, and now he watched and waited for her next move.

But I'm not his wife, she silently insisted. *I am still untouched.*

Jeremiah told her once that love could easily change to hate and hate to murder. Pride usually controlled a man's emotions, especially those affairs of the heart.

Katie had admitted her past love for Lone Eagle. She couldn't deny those feelings or pretend nothing ever happened. Katie realized she had worshipped Lone Eagle. Everything about the Comanche warrior had intrigued her:

his hair—the color of the crow; his deep, penetrating eyes that had always held tenderness for her; the magnificent way he carried himself. Lone Eagle stood for the virtues held high by every tribal member. He fought bravely, and others told of his mighty acts in battle. As Swift Arrow's eldest son, Lone Eagle spent many hours with his father learning how to lead the tribe. His mother loved him above her other children; she sewed for Lone Eagle and cooked his favorite foods. The warrior knew his guardian spirits and regularly consulted their medicine. Comanche families wanted him to notice their daughters and befriend their sons. Lone Eagle rose as a son among sons, a warrior among warriors.

Katie realized her love for Lone Eagle had led her to believe he was perfect. Lone Eagle did have a bad temper and a vindictive nature. How could she have overlooked the way he oppressed weaker warriors or shunned Indian maidens who were plain? Jealousy and arrogance clasped hands with Lone Eagle, and he never let her forget he would one day be chief of the Comanches. When they were alone, Lone Eagle showered her with affection. Katie never doubted his love or devotion, but many things had changed since she came to live with Seth and Elizabeth. Her love for Lone Eagle began to diminish when she viewed how the people around her cared for each other. They worshipped the one true God—a God of love and compassion.

God please help me, Katie shuddered. *Because I don't want to ever go back to him.*

੨ॐ

Colonel Ross sent Peyton on another patrol, but Peyton failed to inform Katie; neither did he tell her good-bye. In fact, he purposely avoided her, and Katie found out about the patrol through Lauren. This time the soldiers would be gone a week.

Katie prayed for Peyton's safety and for them to be able to talk upon his return. He had to have made a decision about the two of them by now. Maybe the silence provided an answer.

The ache in her heart refused to go away; she hurt in the mornings and even more at night. Elizabeth and Seth continued their comfort and encouragement. Their wordless gestures told Katie they shared her pain. Katie knew they cared for Peyton, too, and it didn't help when Jacob asked about his soldier.

"Jacob, would you like to go fishing?" Katie asked when the small boy asked again about Sergeant Sinclair.

He didn't need to think twice. "Yes. Can we go now?"

Katie smiled and ruffled his hair. "Of course. I heard Uncle Seth say he had a taste for fish."

"I'll catch them all," Jacob boasted. "And I'll dig for worms."

The day had a bit of chill to it and Katie made sure Jacob wore a coat. Together the two carried poles and a wooden bucket to bring back their catches. Katie hoped the sun would peek through the bleak sky to warm them a little, but the clouds seemed to carry the threat of snow.

Limpia Brook rippled noisily while Katie helped Jacob find worms. She'd tucked in a few slices of bread in case the fish needed encouragement to swallow the line.

"Indian boys catch fish with their hands," she informed Jacob.

He attempted to snatch up a swimming trout, but the fish proved faster than his little hands.

"The water is too cold," Jacob said. "My fingers are froze."

Katie warmed them with her own hands, and soon he was ready to try again.

"Let's try catching fish the Indian way when the weather is warmer," she suggested with a laugh. "Today we can fish like the soldiers and Uncle Seth." Katie handed him a pole, and Jacob took it reluctantly. "I bet my fish will be bigger than yours," she said, and Jacob took her challenge.

An hour passed and still no fish. Jacob was rapidly becoming discouraged, then something nibbled at his line.

"Look, Katie, I've got one," he fairly shouted.

She helped him bring in a good-sized trout and land it in the bucket.

"Now, it's your turn," Jacob insisted, "but I know mine is bigger."

A short time later, Katie brought in one that measured slightly shorter than Jacob's fish.

"You won," she announced. "I think we have enough for supper. Shall we take these two home?"

Jacob nodded. "Yes, I'm cold."

Once inside the fort, Katie heard the sound of soldiers and saw the army patrol enter the front gate. From the distance they looked tired and dusty, but nothing out of the ordinary. Then she spotted two soldiers tied across their saddles, and three others wore makeshift bandages. Peyton wore one of the bandages around his shoulder. From her stance, she saw bloodstains.

"Peyton!" Katie cried, leaving the fish bucket and rushing with Jacob to his side. "You're hurt."

"It's nothing serious, just a shoulder wound," Peyton replied coldly. He had yet to dismount his horse but rather surveyed the crowd. "Some of us weren't so lucky." She couldn't bring herself to look at the dead men, and she realized Jacob did not need to be a part of this crowd. Besides, Peyton's tone didn't invite conversation.

He's still angry, she thought sadly. *And with the deaths and injuries of his men, I can't expect him to want to talk to me.*

Katie stepped back while Peyton grabbed the saddle horn with his left hand and swung his leg around the horse. Awkward, silent moments followed as a crowd formed around all the men. Some asked questions, others helped the wounded and dead. Katie heard a young boy cry out for his pa.

"I'm sorry," Katie said to Peyton.

She looked around to see if anyone needed help, but there were more than enough people assisting the others. She'd just be in the way. Taking a deep breath and breathing a prayer for the soldiers and their families, Katie and Jacob retrieved the bucket and walked home.

Late into the night, Katie woke to the sound of someone pounding on the door. Seth should answer it, especially in light of the hour, but the pounding persisted and she didn't want the children wakened.

"Who would want a horse shod this hour of the night?" Katie whispered to herself as she hurried to the door. "Who's there?" she asked as quietly as possible.

"Peyton."

"Do you have any idea what time it is?" Katie asked, perturbed at his late call.

"Yes, I can't sleep," said the voice behind the door.

"Well, I was sleeping just fine," Katie said, purposely lacing her words with agitation. "What do you want, anyway?"

"To talk to you."

"Peyton Sinclair, are you drunk?"

"No, the doc gave me laudanum for pain, but I didn't drink a thing. Are you coming out to talk?"

"No! I'm not dressed, and it's not proper."

"It's dark out here; no one is going to see. Can't you put on your coat and shoes?"

"Katie," Seth whispered, parting the blanket partition. "Who is out there?"

Katie saw her uncle in the doorway of his room. "It's Peyton," she whispered.

"What does he want?"

"For me to come out there to talk. I've already told him no. I'm not properly dressed, but he won't listen," Katie explained.

"Is he drunk?" Seth asked.

"I already asked him the same thing. He says no."

"Katie, are you coming out?" Peyton called.

Katie shook her head in utter disgust. "Would you hush? You've already wakened Uncle Seth, and if you get these

children up, I'll put a bullet through your other shoulder."
Katie looked over in Seth's direction. "What do I do, Uncle?"

Seth hesitated. "I'll run him off if you want me to. . .aw, go
on out and listen to what he has to say. I'm awake now, so if
he's drunk or bothers you, holler out. I'll thrash him good if
he touches you. Who knows? He may have something worth-
while to say, and it can't wait until morning."

Katie lifted the latch and stepped out into the cold air.
She'd grabbed her coat and pulled on her shoes. Soft, wet
flakes of snow sifted through the dark and rested on her
hands.

"It's snowing," Peyton remarked casually.

"I know, the first one this year. Is this why you came to see
me?" Katie asked, feeling exasperated with his conversation.

"No, Katie. I've come on serious business."

Katie wished she could see his face, maybe then she could
tell his mood. "Be quick about it, Peyton. I'm freezing."

"The last time we talked, things weren't finished," Peyton
began.

"I well remember our conversation," Katie said, wrapping
her arms around herself.

"Do you want me to keep you warm?" Peyton asked.

"No. And if you think you can get by with a thing, Uncle
Seth is waiting inside to thrash you," Katie warned.

Peyton must have thought her remark incredibly funny,
because he broke into a fit of laughter.

"Would you hush before you wake the entire fort," Katie
said. "I swear, if I find out you're drunk, I will. . .I will. . ."

"Scalp me?" Peyton asked.

"Now, that's not funny. I'm going back inside."

Peyton grabbed her arm, and the sudden movement obviously caused a surge of fire to his injured shoulder.

Katie gasped as she heard him wince with the pain. "Are
you sure you should be out with your shoulder?" Katie asked.

Instantly Peyton's tone changed. "It's a little sore, but it will be all right. I'm sorry, Katie. Please, wait a minute more. I need to talk to you."

Katie tapped her foot against the cold ground. "Go ahead, I'm listening."

"I've had lots of time to think about the two of us, and I have a few things to say," he said.

Katie's heart beat wildly against her chest. For the first time since she came outside, she was glad for the blackness of night.

Peyton continued. "First, I love you and nothing is going to change that. Second, I'm as pigheaded and stubborn as you are." Katie smiled in the dark. "Third, I want to force Lone Eagle's hand on this. I think we can make him state his intentions about you. It's risky, but I can't expect you to marry me until I know you are free to be my wife."

Katie said nothing while she reflected upon Peyton's words. "What do you suggest?" she finally asked.

"Let's announce our engagement," he said in one breath. "The Kiowa is here; he said he needed to purchase provisions. We can be certain the message will get back to Lone Eagle."

"What if he orders you killed?" Katie asked quietly.

"I'll risk it. Besides, I can't live without you."

"Now, who is being noble?" Katie asked, without a trace of humor. "Oh, I don't know what to say, Peyton. I want this finished with Lone Eagle, but I'm afraid for you."

"I've prayed about it," Peyton said simply. "It doesn't do any good to argue with a praying man, especially one who is in love."

"I've prayed about us, too," Katie said. "All right, I'll agree to your plan, and we'll wait for Lone Eagle's next move."

"We will be better at waiting than he is because we have God on our side," Peyton said, and Katie heard the conviction in his voice.

She would be a fool not to admit the alarm and fright washing over her whole body. Katie shivered, but not from the cold. Peyton's plan brought the whole nightmare to a peak. She shouldn't have agreed. Peyton could be killed; she could be killed or forced to spend the rest of her life with the Comanche warrior.

Lone Eagle's decision still held Peyton and Katie's future, but God held their destiny. No matter what happened in the weeks ahead, God would be with them. He knew their hearts, and He would protect them. Katie remembered the search for her rehoboth, and a peculiar peace settled upon her.

Trust Me, Katie. Let Me guide you.

thirteen

When Katie stepped back inside the cabin, she found Seth rocking Emily.

"I leaned over to kiss her and woke her up," Seth whispered sheepishly. "What did the sergeant want at this late hour?"

Katie smiled warmly in the dark. "He asked me to marry him."

Seth could barely contain his jubilance. Little Emily opened her eyes wide and sat up in his lap. "Now look what I've done," he said with a chuckle.

Elizabeth appeared at their side, and Katie repeated the story to her. Her aunt immediately burst into tears and insisted she didn't think it right to give up one of her children so soon.

"But if you have to leave us, at least it's to a fine young man," Elizabeth said, hugging Katie close.

"I declare," Seth said. "I thought the man had indulged himself in too much whiskey, but instead he was drunk with love. And here I sat ready to teach him a lesson. He *is* a good man, Katie, and I'm proud to call him a son-in-law. I must be getting old, because I forgot he asked permission to marry you right after you two had your last spat. I should have known."

Katie could hardly believe her uncle's words.

"Yes, Katie, child. The sergeant came to me the day before he left on patrol and asked if he could have your hand in marriage," Seth explained.

In the next few days news spread quickly through the community, and Peyton and Katie met head-on all of the questions surrounding the engagement. The two decided upon a Christmas wedding with the ceremony set for the afternoon of December 24. In less than six weeks, Peyton and Katie would be man and wife. It also meant Lone Eagle had less than six weeks to respond to the news.

"What if Lone Eagle chooses to do nothing about our marriage?" Katie asked one evening after they had announced their plans. The two walked hand in hand back from a visit with Reverend Cooper. All day her excitement had mounted, and she had tried to discount it in light of Peyton's reasons for an early wedding date. Katie knew Peyton loved her, but she regretted the reason for the ceremony centered on Lone Eagle.

"Then I get a wife for Christmas," he stated.

"I don't want you to feel like you have to go through with this ceremony," Katie said. "I feel like Lone Eagle is the reason you want to get married."

Peyton stopped, and with his uninjured hand, lifted her chin. "Lone Eagle is the reason I hadn't asked before. I needed to be sure you weren't still in love with him."

Katie felt warm tears stinging her eyes. "Oh, Peyton, I don't deserve your love. I will love you and be a good wife, I promise you."

Peyton leaned over and kissed her lightly on the nose. "Now, are there any more questions filling your pretty little head?"

"Yes, I have a lot of them. Where will we live?" Katie asked.

"Let me think," Peyton mused. "Since it's Christmas Eve, I could ask the colonel to let us use part of the stable. The animals could keep us warm. Seems fittin', don't you agree?"

"I'm serious," Katie said, wanting to punch him but fearing she might hurt his wounded shoulder.

"So am I! Truthfully, I have my eye on an empty cabin near the end of the civilian section. It needs a new roof and some fixin' up, but I can do it."

"Are you sure this is really what you want?" Katie asked with mixed emotions.

Peyton's answer came in a kiss.

"I want the two of us married and raising a bunch of kids. I want to grow old with you and see our grandchildren play together. We will have a beautiful life together, but not until Lone Eagle releases his hold on you," Peyton said firmly.

"What will we do if Lone Eagle puts me into a position where I have to go back to him?" Katie asked more calmly than she felt.

"You aren't going back to him," Peyton said. "Colonel Ross is the only one who knows about this. I've confided in him, and he has helped me devise a plan to capture Lone Eagle. This territory will be free of his murdering raids, and I will have Katie Colter as my wife."

&

With the early wedding date, Elizabeth grumbled and pointed out the lack of necessary items in Katie's trousseau. Peyton hadn't given her enough notice to plan a wedding or prepare things to take up housekeeping. Elizabeth warned Peyton to prepare for a lecture every day until the wedding.

Many folks congratulated the young couple; even some of those who normally criticized Katie now smiled politely. The contrary Mrs. Ames even made a point of stopping after church to give her congratulations.

"If I had known so many people would be nice to you, I would have asked you to marry me the moment you rode into the fort," Peyton said after Katie received a gift of canned fruit from Mrs. Ames.

"In one breath, I'm so excited about the wedding," Katie said. "But in the next breath, I'm afraid of Lone Eagle's response. We shouldn't have to make wedding preparations around a threat."

"You're right and I agree totally with you, except we know God's hand is on our marriage. I don't believe God wants us to spend the rest of our lives wondering what Lone Eagle might or might not do. Our wedding date merely forces Lone Eagle to make a decision. Sweetheart, it's the only choice we have."

Katie nodded, realizing every word he spoke was the truth. "When would you have proposed if Lone Eagle hadn't been a threat?" she asked.

Peyton chuckled. "There's a whole lot of wisdom in proposing to a girl in the middle of a cold dark night. My timing would probably be the same. You would either have to say yes or freeze until you did. Lone Eagle had nothing to do with my proposal."

But Katie knew differently.

Peyton made certain the Kiowa heard the news. Within a week, the Indian disappeared from the fort. The young couple waited for Lone Eagle's reply.

Well-wishers invited the engaged couple to dinner, and Lauren and Martha stitched furiously on those special linens required in a young lady's trousseau. Katie searched through her trunk of belongings and found her mother's wedding dress. It fit perfectly with no alterations, and Katie wondered if anyone else ever knew such happiness. With tears, which seemed to dampen her face much more than usual, Katie thought how wonderful it would have been to have her mother see her marry. The emotion rose again when she asked Seth to give her away. How she missed her father.

&

"Katie, I want to get out of the army," Peyton announced.

Katie reflected upon his statement. It sounded like an answer to prayer. "Good," she said simply. "I worry so each time you ride out. My fears seem to chip away at my heart."

"Well, my enlistment is up in the spring, and I think I'm ready to settle down into civilian life again."

"What do you want to do?" Katie asked.

This time Peyton paused reflectively. "I'd like to visit my folks in Illinois, and, of course, let them get to know my beautiful wife. I haven't seen them or my brothers in over five years. I miss them, and it seems right to go home for a visit."

"What then?"

"I've been thinking that God may want me to finish medical school."

"Oh my, I've never heard you say anything about wanting to be a doctor," she said curiously.

"Well," he began. "It's why I joined the army. It's a long story, but one I suppose you need to hear." Peyton rubbed his bandaged shoulder. Lately the wound had started to itch with its healing. "My folks wanted me to be a doctor, so to please them, I attended two years of medical school. I'd never been so miserable in my whole life. I thought the only thing I ever wanted to do was come out west and take up ranching. I sank into a horrible depression, and that was when an old friend of my father's talked to me about the Lord. Well, the hope in his message and the words of grace and mercy made me realize I needed a Savior. It didn't take long for me to give my life over to the Lord. My folks were elated. Not only were they going to have a doctor in the family, but they also had a Christian. It took a lot of courage to tell them of my decision to leave school. They were hurt and very disappointed. So I joined the army to give all of us time to heal. The trouble is I never saw a clear picture of what God intended for me until I met you. Then everything moved into place. I hope you will like being a doctor's wife, 'cause my mind is pretty set on it. I've saved enough money to buy us a small home and get me started back at school."

"But Peyton," Katie interrupted. "I have a ranch," she said eagerly. "It's green and fertile and is bound to bring a good price."

Peyton looked at her oddly. "I forgot about your father's place."

"Our place," Katie corrected. "I could sell it, and then I'd have a perfect trousseau."

"Do you want to give up your land?"

"Of course—it should belong to someone who could raise

cattle and horses. My pa used to talk about building a cattle ranch, but it never happened. I don't want to raise our children in Indian territory. I want them some place safe. We've both seen enough tragedy in this land to last forever."

Katie saw the idea had a sobering effect upon Peyton. "What's wrong, Peyton? Is it because the land is mine?"

"No, sweetheart. With my savings, we can start better than I expected."

Katie wanted so much to marry Peyton and spend the rest of her life with him. To live out their lives without the fear of raiding Indians seemed almost too good to be true. God had blessed her with a good man, one who loved her dearly and demonstrated his compassion and gentleness in countless ways. Peyton would make an excellent doctor. How proud she felt! Now if Lone Eagle would just leave them alone so they could start their life together.

Peyton knew Katie couldn't promise she would not go back to Lone Eagle if he forced a life and death decision. Lone Eagle most likely knew that, too. Perhaps she did appear selfish in wanting to shield those she loved, but she would feel much more selfish if she rebelled against Lone Eagle's demands and caused innocent people to suffer. She couldn't run away, and she couldn't marry Peyton without Lone Eagle releasing her commitment to him. Waiting and praying seemed to be all Katie could do, but it didn't seem to be enough. Katie wanted to do something, anything to force Lone Eagle to make a stand.

God, isn't there anything big or small I can do to hurry this along? I hate waiting, God. I don't know what Lone Eagle is thinking or what he wants from me. Am I being self-centered? Could it be my worries are needless? Help me to give it all to you and not keep pulling it back. Thank you for Peyton; he's so good to me.

Katie took a deep breath and asked God to forgive her for rambling. The truth of the matter was she feared Peyton's plan might get Lone Eagle killed or worse yet, Peyton. She had no desire for the warrior to die; the idea sickened her. How could she want him dead? Lone Eagle had been her first love; and even though she had been naive and foolish, the feelings were real. The warrior said he loved her, and Katie had believed she loved him. Despite all of the horrible injustices he had done, Lone Eagle had shown her a tender side. Nothing excused his murdering raids, but the good things about him did deserve a soft portion of her heart. Katie desperately needed him to reconsider his claims upon her.

With all her heart, Katie felt the whites and the Indians could live together if they tried to understand each other and make compromises. Honor and respect could prevail in the land if each promised to abide by a given set of rules. Katie refused to think of any more killing for either Indian or whites.

Trust Me, Katie.

fourteen

The chill in the air, the festivities of Christmas, and all of the excitement of the wedding lifted Katie and Peyton's spirits. Neither wanted to concentrate on the gravity of the situation before them or discuss it. Ignoring Lone Eagle did not eliminate the problem, it merely postponed it. The Kiowa would arrive soon enough with the warrior's message. Katie decided to enjoy the celebrations of the season and the preparations for their new home as long as possible. She repeatedly told herself it did little good to worry and decided to say nothing unless Peyton mentioned it. Except each time Peyton wanted to speak of it, Katie refused to talk. Denial had never been a part of Katie's makeup, but she felt compelled to push their problems away.

The two worked side by side preparing the cabin. With Miles and Lauren's help, they replaced the roof and muddied up the sides to keep out the cold. But there were times Peyton drifted into silence, and Katie didn't question his moods.

"I think we should name all of our children from people in the Bible," Katie suggested one evening as they finished sealing the cracks inside the cabin. Peyton had built a fire, and the small structure felt warm and comfortable.

"Well, I had a different idea," Peyton informed her.

Katie stopped with her small bucket of mud mixed with straw and eyed him curiously. "What did you have in mind?"

"I was thinking that I wanted our children to always remember their mother and grandfather once lived with the Indians," he said, continuing his work.

"And?"

"So I would like to name them after Indian tribes. The first

120

one we'd call Comanche, then Apache—that sounds good for a girl, ah yes and Kiowa, Sioux—another girl's name, Navajo, Black Foot, Cheyenne, and on until we get a dozen or so."

Katie stood speechless. "Peyton, are you crazy? Why ever would you want to give a child such a name?"

"I like the sound of 'em. You know, those names just seem to roll off the tongue. For certain, all the folks would know the Sinclair children."

"That's for sure," Katie said dryly. "Let's talk about this. I bet we could come up with good names that both of us would like."

"Nope, my mind is made up," Peyton said with his back to her. "I've already entered a few in my Bible."

"No, you haven't," Katie accused, suddenly aware of his teasing. "You're tormenting me again. You should be ashamed."

"Me?" Peyton whirled around with mud on his fingers and a glint in his eye. "I have more: Cado, Iroquois, Cherokee. . ."

"You will never be able to convince me of those names," she said in pretended annoyance.

Peyton stepped closer, threatening her with mud-covered fingers, but he stole a kiss instead. "I might reconsider after the first dozen."

❧

Katie insisted upon helping Martha and Lauren with school during the mornings. The children made gifts for their parents, and one morning they all made sugar cookies. They rehearsed Christmas carols to sing on Christmas Eve as a part of the wedding and again later for church services. Their sweet voices always brought tears to Katie's eyes, even when the bigger boys grumbled about singing. During lunch she hurried back to the cabin while Jacob stayed with the other students until midafternoon. The hours sped by quickly as she and Elizabeth took turns caring for Emily, discussing the wedding, and tending to chores.

This morning Martha and Lauren insisted Katie return home

and work on sewing projects for her new home. Martha reminded her that there were only two weeks left until the wedding. The cabin still needed work, and she looked tired. Needless to say, many items remained to be stitched and sewn.

Katie lifted the latch on the Colter cabin and quietly stepped inside. She had so many things on her mind, and Emily might be resting. She heard the sound of voices in Seth and Elizabeth's bedroom. It seemed odd for Seth to be home in the middle of the day. Unlike other settlers at the fort, his position as blacksmith kept him busy while others searched for chores to keep occupied. Katie hoped her uncle had not become ill.

"Seth, you can't put this off any longer," Katie heard Elizabeth state firmly. "She needs to be told the truth."

"I know, I know, but you have no idea what you're asking of me," Seth said wearily.

"I realize you have lived with this for over seventeen years," Elizabeth said gently. "But it's time to put the past behind you. Katie loves you, just as you love her."

"She will despise me if I tell her the truth. Katie thinks I'm a God-fearing man, when in fact I'm vile and loathsome."

"No, you're not," Elizabeth said sharply. "You're good and kind and decent. Seth Colter, don't let the guilt hurt you any longer. This thing has eaten at you for too long. It's time to get it out in the open. Both of you love each other, and God will work it out."

"She's about to be married in two weeks' time," Seth said. "Why do I need to tell her at all? She'll have a husband, and they will be gone in the spring."

Katie pushed aside the blanket separating the two rooms. "Tell me what, Uncle Seth? What could be so dreadful that you don't want to tell me?"

Katie saw the injured look pass from her uncle to her aunt.

"I'll do it," Seth whispered to his wife. "It's about time I took responsibility for my own mistakes." Seth reached for

Katie, and she gave him her hand. "We need to talk, Katie child. There's some things you need to hear."

Seth pointed to the chair, and Katie took her place. A chill had swept across the room, and she pulled the quilt from the back of the chair and laid it across her lap. Once Elizabeth left the room, Seth seated himself on the side of the bed. Katie saw he looked pale and much older.

"Uncle Seth, are you ill? Would you like this quilt?" Katie asked.

"No, dear. I'm not ill, at least not in my flesh."

She gazed at him, puzzled, and the troubled look on his face caused her concern.

"This is real hard," Seth began. "And there's no easy way to say it. I won't make excuses for myself or expect you to understand. I just hope you will be able to forgive me."

"Forgive you for what?"

Seth leaned slightly toward her, and she saw his eyes moisten. "Jeremiah, my brother. . .was not your father. I am."

Seth's words echoed in her ears, hollow and empty. Her stomach churned, and she drew the quilt up tightly around her. Katie refused to believe him; surely Seth had made a mistake. *How can this be? Jeremiah Colter wasn't her father! This can't be possible.* And her mother, so sweet and gentle. . . What did this mean?

Seth must have seen the shock and pain in Katie's face for he instantly chose to speak. "Child, neither was Mary Colter your mother. Your real mother died of pneumonia before you were six months old."

It couldn't be true. Why wasn't she ever told? Folks said she looked like Mary and even had some of her mannerisms. Jeremiah and Mary Colter were not her parents! Yes, they were; she knew they were. This had to be a dreadful nightmare. Seth had made a terrible mistake. How could he explain those years Jeremiah raised her by himself? If she didn't belong to Jeremiah, then why didn't he send her to Seth and

Elizabeth when Mary died? If her uncle spoke the truth, then why hadn't Jeremiah told her about it? She was grown and had the right to know. Why did Jeremiah speak of rehoboth and not of this horrible revelation?

Katie lifted her chin and swallowed the lump in her throat. "I don't understand what you're saying. I'm so confused."

"I should have told you the truth when you came to live with us, but I feared losing you."

Katie took a deep breath. "How did this happen? Why didn't anyone ever tell me?"

Seth shook his head as though denying the past. "I promised not to ever interfere with your life—never claim you as my daughter. I didn't think anything would ever happen to Mary and Jeremiah to leave you alone."

"Please, will you explain it all to me?"

Silence followed, and Katie fought the twisting and turning in the pit of her stomach. She looked into the face of her uncle, a face marred with the lines of sadness. Seth sighed deeply. His eyes cast a faraway glance, and he appeared to look through her to another time and place.

"The first time I met your mother was on Mary and Jeremiah's wedding day. Mary introduced Hannah as her younger sister, and I instantly fell in love with the most beautiful girl in the world. I'll never forget the first time I looked into those huge jade green eyes and met that sweet smile. She looked like an angel straight from heaven's gate. Katie, every part of you is Hannah, your real mother. Looking at you is like seeing her again for the first time." With Hannah's name upon his lips, Seth's face brightened. "Anyway, I wanted to court her proper, but her pa refused until she turned sixteen. For weeks I marked off the days until I could start seein' her. She became the reason I lived and breathed. I couldn't think or talk for thinking about her. Soon afterwards I asked her pa if we could marry, but he said we would have to wait until she reached seventeen. Again, I began marking off those weeks until her birthday. At last we were married, and our lives seemed perfect. I thought we were the happiest two people on earth."

Katie saw Seth struggle to gain composure. Her own feelings oscillated from anger to hurt, but when she saw the agony etched across Seth's face, compassion overcame any desire to hurl accusations.

"Please go on," Katie said, swallowing her tears. "Not just what you think I should hear, but all of it. If you are my real father, then I must know what happened. All of my life, they told me they loved me. Neither of them ever let on that I wasn't their own child."

"They did love you, Katie. Don't you ever doubt Jeremiah and Mary's devotion to you. I remember the day you were born. Why, those two were as happy as we were. Then my Hannah took sick with a cold and fever; then it got worse. Before long, she couldn't get out of bed. One morning I woke up and Hannah lay beside me, not breathing but cold and still. I wanted to die myself. I turned my back on everything in this life, including you. In those days, I didn't know Jesus, so I blamed God for all my heartache. Child, everyday you looked more like your mother, and instead of seeing it as a blessing, I saw it as a horrible reminder of not having Hannah. I took you to Jeremiah and Mary and asked them to raise you. In turn, I promised to never claim you as my daughter. It sounded simple, the best way to handle my grief.

"Jeremiah had always been the restless type—couldn't seem to get roots back home. He wanted adventure, and he loved the wild. All the education in the world couldn't satisfy his longing for it. He wanted to take his family west and carve out a home for them. Mary loved Jeremiah. She was afraid to head out across the wilderness, but she wouldn't try to stop him. No sooner had they arrived than Jeremiah wrote, asking me to join them. He wanted me to see the beauty of his new home. Jeremiah told me about traveling through mountains and deserts until he found this piece of fertile land along the Teyah

River. His letter went on and on about the animals, birds, sunrises, sunsets, the mountains, and his fascination with the Indians. For my benefit, he added that a few families had settled into an area a few miles away, so the territory wasn't completely desolate. My brother knew my blacksmith abilities would be valuable to those folks. It sounded good to me, so I gathered up my belongings and moved out here. My first reaction to this dangerous land, filled with rattlesnakes and Indians, didn't compare to Jeremiah's, but I stayed. Yes, it's beautiful, but not quite what I had expected. Sometimes I thought he had gone crazy to bring you and Mary to such a godforsaken territory, but Jeremiah had never been happier. He'd made friends with the Comanches, Apaches, and Kiowas. He traded with them so he and Mary weren't bothered by raids. Some of the other settlers didn't like his way of mixing with the Indians. They criticized him rather than listened to his way of thinking. As a result, Jeremiah stopped visiting the settlers, not that I blamed him. It made sense when he spoke of respecting the Indians, and he believed they were smarter than the white man when it came to survival.

"Both Mary and Jeremiah asked me to move in with them, but I refused. I'd long since regretted giving you to them, and it hurt too much to consider seeing you everyday. Besides, I had a business, and folks weren't about to risk their lives to see a blacksmith. If I wanted to see the three of you, I had to travel to their ranch." Seth stood from the bed. Silently, he paced across the small room.

"I want to hear what happened next," Katie urged.

Seth seated himself again, and Katie watched him wrestle with the words and the memories. "Two years later, I met Elizabeth. I don't know what she saw in me, but thank God she took the time to care. In those days, I was a miserable, short-tempered man, and Hannah still filled my waking and sleeping hours. I had nightmares where she repeatedly called out for you. Guilt began to eat away at me for what I'd done.

One night I told Elizabeth the whole truth, and instead of condemning me, she told me about God and His wonderful love. Elizabeth explained how His Son took on the sins of the world so that I might one day live in heaven. He wanted to forgive my sins and set me free from the guilt and blame of abandoning my daughter. Before the evening ended, Elizabeth led me to Jesus. For the first time, I felt a flow of peace and love that softened my heart and opened my eyes to all of the bitterness eating away at me. Elizabeth and I talked for hours. She helped me see that God had decided Hannah needed to be with Him, and it wasn't my fault or yours. Yet, I would have to abide by the promise I made to allow Jeremiah and Mary to raise my daughter. A few months later, I asked Elizabeth to marry me. Jeremiah and Mary immediately saw the change, and both of them began asking questions and studying the Bible. I thanked the both of them for what they were doing for my daughter and asked them to forgive me for all the trouble I'd caused. After Mary died, I asked Jeremiah for you, but he refused. He said you were his, and he would never give you up. . .and then he died."

Silence filled the room. Katie heard the chatter of Jacob, and once Emily cried out, but Seth's words spun like a child's toy in her mind.

"I need some time to myself," Katie said, avoiding Seth's stare.

"I understand."

"I need to think through everything you told me. I don't know what else to say."

"Neither do I."

"Uncle, I. . .I mean, goodness I'm terribly mixed up," Katie said, fighting to keep her composure.

Seth stood, but she couldn't look into his face. "Saying I'm sorry isn't enough, and asking you to forgive me doesn't seem like enough either. Reckon, I'll let you alone."

fifteen

Katie swept the remains of the dirt and debris from the small cabin she would soon call home. Outside the temperatures steadily dropped, and along with the wintry chill fell a heavy blanket of snow. Katie held her breath against the sharp cold and surveyed the new roof. Miles and Seth had been so good to help Peyton, or the work would not have been completed in time to stop the wind from searching for a hole in the cabin. Inside, the cabin needed only a few more repairs to make it livable for her and Peyton. She should have been elated, but her mood more closely resembled the dark, gray snow clouds lingering above Fort Davis. Stepping back inside to the warmth of the crackling fire, she watched the flaming swords shoot upward as they snatched up dry pieces of wood and consumed them into burning ash.

"What's wrong?" Peyton asked. He'd been hammering pegs to hang pots, pans, and other items necessary for cooking. Now he gave Katie his full attention.

"I can't keep anything from you," Katie said, attempting to sound light, but the weight of her thoughts pulled away the joy she always felt with him. She examined his work as though her concentration had been solely upon his wooden pegs.

"Sweetheart, your face shows your feelings."

"True Comanches don't reveal their emotions," Katie remarked casually.

"Oh, I can recall many times when you hid behind your stubborn resolve," Peyton said. "For example, I thought you tolerated me for your uncle's sake." He looked at her oddly. "This is serious, isn't it?"

She stepped into his arms and slipped her hands around his

neck. "We need to talk," she said grimly. "Or maybe I just need for you to listen. A part of me wants to cry and another part wants to scream and shout."

"Sit with me by the fire," Peyton said. He motioned to a buffalo hide spread out beneath him and pulled her to the floor. "Have you heard from the Kiowa, sweetheart?"

"No, this is completely different from our problem with Lone Eagle," Katie said. "Seth told me something earlier today that has me really upset."

"I can see you're grieved about something," Peyton said, placing his arm around her shoulders. "Are you ready to talk?"

"I'm going to try," Katie said, and she proceeded to tell him about the conversation with Seth.

"Do you despise him for what he told you?" Peyton asked once she finished.

"No, I'm not sure what I'm feeling, but it's not hate. Look at all the good he's done for me. I couldn't even begin to list all those things. Without him, I wouldn't have received Jesus into my life or understood many passages from the Bible. He has fed me and clothed me—asking nothing in return. And Peyton, you are the only man he gave permission to come calling. I guess I'm saddened to learn the perfect picture of my parents is tainted."

"Are you looking for someone to blame because you weren't told the truth?"

"Maybe, but I care about all of them. That's the worst of the problem. I can't seem to think things through." Katie rested her head on his shoulder.

"How do you feel about Jeremiah?" Peyton continued gently, and Katie realized his questioning was to help her sort out her own feelings.

"I loved him," Katie said gently. "He raised me as his own daughter and always told me how proud he was of me. He used to call me his Indian princess."

"What about Mary?"

"I think she must have loved my mother very much to take me into her heart. It seems so tragic that Mary died while giving birth to her own child."

"Do you think Jeremiah and Mary regretted raising you as their own?"

Katie paused; even though Seth had assured her of their love, she wanted to make sure she agreed with him. "No, I am very sure they loved me. I remember the laughter and the good times we had together. Pa often brought us wildflowers, and Ma always made a big fuss. He liked to hear her sing, and she always had a song. Sometimes late at night, they would sit out on the front porch and Ma would sing. He would come and lift me from my bed and hold me in his lap until the precious sound of her voice lulled me to sleep. Yes, Peyton, I'm sure they loved me."

"So, does knowing Seth Colter is your real father change the feelings you have for any of them?"

Katie wiped the tears from her cheeks. "No, I guess not. If anything I should love them more for their devotion to me and keeping the secret. If I consider it all, Seth could have made my life miserable when I came here, but he put aside the past and welcomed me into his home. Today he told me that seeing me was like looking at my mother again. And then I consider Elizabeth, who could have resented me and sent me back to the Comanches, but she loves me, too."

"You might want to tell Seth those exact words," Peyton said, taking her hand.

"I know I should, but I feel so strange and uncomfortable knowing he is my real father and that I never knew my mother. I am sure I can forgive my father for giving me up, but it will take some getting used to."

Peyton toyed with her fingers, then kissed them lightly. "Katie, Seth Colter made a mistake when he gave you to Jeremiah and Mary, but they loved Seth and Hannah and chose to make you a blessing. In his pain, Seth believed he could live his life as your uncle. He gave his word to ensure that very thing. He may have been grieving, yet he recognized his child needed a good home. Then he came to know the Lord, and his commitment to Jeremiah and Mary demonstrated real love. His feelings for you went far beyond the baby given to his brother and wife. Seth knew real love, an unselfish giving for the benefit of others. I'm sure it bothered him every day of his life, and I'm even more sure God became his only source of comfort and peace."

"Peyton, you always see things so clearly," Katie said wistfully.

"Not really. I'm a stubborn man, and I want things to go my way, but I pray God always puts me back on the right path."

Katie contemplated Peyton's words. She couldn't ignore the truth or deny Seth's confession. Their relationship might be awkward, but it was up to her to take the next step.

"You're right, Peyton. If God doesn't judge Seth, and He has forgiven him, I should do the same."

"Why don't you let me finish up here, and you can go see him?" Peyton suggested.

"Oh, it would be so difficult. I don't know if I am ready to face him," Katie protested.

"The longer you wait, the harder it will be."

Katie understood exactly what Peyton meant. She didn't want a wall built between her and Seth, neither did she want Jeremiah and Mary's memory tarnished with bitterness. Katie recalled Seth telling her that forgiveness leads to freedom. The truth didn't change Jeremiah and Mary's love for her; it confirmed it.

Katie stood from her place beside Peyton. "I'll go now," she said. "One of my fathers needs to know I love him."

"Do you want me to go with you?" he asked.

"No, I should do this myself. . .Peyton?"

"Yes."

"I'm still amazed at how you always manage to see things so clearly."

Peyton laughed and broke the seriousness of the moment. "It's much easier to tell someone else how to handle their problems than to solve your own. Remember, I ran away from mine? I joined the army rather than face my family's disappointment over my decision to leave medical school."

"You and I seem to face one ugly situation after another," Katie said. "Do you suppose our lives will ever smooth out?"

"I hope so," Peyton said soberly. "Right now I'm praying we can get through the next two weeks."

And Katie clearly saw the worried lines across his forehead. The Kiowa must come soon.

❧

Katie heard the pounding of Seth's hammer shaping a piece of metal into something useful. She stopped to listen and noted the rhythm sounded faster than usual. Perhaps Seth had too much work to do and didn't have time to speak with her, or he might feel the blacksmith wasn't a fitting place to talk about delicate matters. She could easily put off this conversation until another time.

Katie forced herself to walk into the pathway of the three-sided structure that housed the blacksmith. The forge felt warm, and she knew without looking that Seth's face would be red from the heat. At first he didn't see her, but the late afternoon sun cast her shadow in his path. Both of them held back a greeting as though any utterance of words might be interpreted as cold or angry.

"Did you want to see me?" Seth finally asked, breaking the deafening silence.

"Yes, if you are not too busy," Katie said.

"No, Katie child, I always have time for you. Please come inside and warm yourself."

Now she understood why Elizabeth and Seth always referred

to her as Katie child. Katie stepped farther into the black-smith, welcoming the warmth and praying for her words to come easily.

"I've been thinking and talking to Peyton about what you told me," Katie began. "The news is still a shock, but it doesn't or shouldn't change how I feel about you or anyone else. I love you dearly, and I don't want uncomfortable feelings between us. If forgiveness is what you ask, then I forgive you. The things you told me will take some time to get used to, but I'm willing to accept them as part of the past."

"I can't ask for more than love and forgiveness," Seth said. "I wish I could make what happened easier for you to bear."

"It's just going to take time. . .I gather you won't want any-one else to know about this, so I won't tell a soul."

"Well, I don't want things to remain the same. Is that what you want?" Seth asked. A furrow inched across his brow.

Katie shook her head. "I don't know. I mean, you are my father, not my uncle Seth, and my head is filled with ques-tions about my mother."

"I know this is soon, but would you consider calling me Papa, maybe not right now, but later on, when you are more settled about it all?"

Katie searched Seth's face. *This is my father, my real father.* "I like the sound of it, especially when Jacob calls you Papa," she said pensively. "I called my—other father—Pa, so Papa would be different. What if folks ask why I stopped referring to you as uncle?"

"I don't care about other folks. Over seventeen years have gone by without me being able to claim my daughter, and I intend to make up for lost time."

"All right, then Papa it is. Will you still give me away at the wedding?"

Tears formed in Seth's eyes. He set his tools aside, peeled off his gloves, and welcomed Katie into his arms.

Over the next few days, Katie felt a mixture of sadness and

grief as she dealt with the truth. She mentally rehearsed calling Seth Papa, but her resolve didn't stop tense moments when she allowed her mind to slip back to the mother she never knew. At those times, Katie sought out her newfound father and together they laughed and cried about Hannah Colter. Katie learned from Elizabeth some of Mary Colter's own words regarding the love she held for her adopted daughter. To the best of Elizabeth's knowledge, Mary never knew Elizabeth had been told the truth about Katie. For certain the Colter brothers grew into men of integrity.

Events and happenings of Jeremiah's last days and Seth's initial response to her now made sense. Jeremiah rightfully sent her to Seth when he realized impending death would not allow him to fulfill his responsibilities to Katie. She wondered if his instructions to find her rehoboth meant learning the truth about her parents. If so, Katie's search had ended.

Katie recalled when Seth learned of her arrival, he left his blacksmith and welcomed her into his home. Now she understood his tears, his patience with her struggle with God, and his careful discernment of a proper suitor. Elizabeth had encouraged her to seek out Seth's council on matters of importance. Now it all made sense. She smiled each time she recalled the night Seth stood ready to thrash Peyton if he talked or acted in an unseemly way. It was also the night he referred to Peyton as a good son-in-law. At the time, Katie thought Seth merely used the term as a way of expressing his fondness for Peyton.

≈

Christmas and the wedding rapidly approached, and Katie willingly pushed aside the confusion of her origin. She frantically stitched and fashioned Christmas gifts for Elizabeth, Seth, the children, and Peyton. After much deliberation, she decided to sew a deerskin jacket from the pile of hides in the bottom of her trunk. She was so pleased with the results that she took another piece and made a vest for Seth and a smaller one for Jacob. There were embroidered handkerchiefs and a bonnet for Elizabeth and a muslin face doll for Emily. The gifts might have been a bit extravagant, but this was her first real Christmas since Mary died, and it was the Christmas of her wedding. Next year she and Peyton might be living in Illinois and unable to spend the holiday with Seth, Elizabeth, and the children.

Always, in the darkest part of Katie's mind, there lived the threat of Lone Eagle destroying all of their hopes and dreams. Only Peyton shared her fears, and the two planned for their future as though the warrior's threat was hollow. At times Katie wondered if she should speak more with Peyton about Lone Eagle, but she didn't want to spoil the excitement or dampen his enthusiasm. The Kiowa had not shown his face in weeks.

sixteen

"Is everything finished for tomorrow?" Elizabeth asked as she stirred a bowl filled with batter for honey cakes.

"Yes, ma'am, I've got things in order at the cabin and here," Katie replied. "I'm all ready to take up housekeeping."

Elizabeth went through the list of all the items that needed to be in place and completed for the wedding and the reception.

"Tonight I'll finish the pies, and Martha says she has two cakes ready. Lauren and her sisters will help serve, and oh, I nearly forgot—Mrs. Ames brought by a huge apple cobbler. Let's see now. . .tablecloths are clean; so are all of the cups for the punch."

"Hopefully it will warm up tomorrow. I detest the thought of guests leaving early, but I'm afraid they are going to get cold," Elizabeth said. "Of course, having the reception here and at your cabin will help."

"It's simply going to be wonderful," Katie said. She picked up Emily and whirled her around the room. "Won't it be grand? And then Christmas is the very next day! Oh, Elizabeth, I am so happy."

"Your mother—both your mothers—would have loved seeing you so beautiful and full of life," Elizabeth said with a sad smile.

"They can see me," Katie said. "We just can't see them."

"I guess you're right. For certain, you are going to be the loveliest bride this fort has ever seen. Seth is about to burst, and he's invited absolutely everyone."

Katie laughed. "Well, he didn't invite Mrs. Ames, because I did. She promised me she would be here."

Katie danced across the room with Emily, all the while

humming a lively tune. "You know what?" Katie asked. "I'd like to go riding this afternoon."

"Child, it's too cold for a pleasure ride."

"Not really. That's how Jeremiah and I used to celebrate Christmas. We would go for a long ride, then he would give me my gift."

"But it's not possible. There's no one to go with you," Elizabeth pointed out. "Seth is working long hours to finish shoeing horses for the colonel, and Peyton is busy with drills."

"Peyton is off duty from this afternoon through Christmas Day. Colonel Ross called it a wedding present," Katie said with her eyes sparkling. She continued to dance across the room, and Emily enjoyed every minute of it.

"Is Peyton aware of your riding adventure?" Elizabeth asked in pretended annoyance. "Or is this a surprise for him, too?"

"He knows, although his reaction was similar to yours. He will be here shortly to see if I am allowed to go."

Elizabeth shook her head and pointed to Emily's need to be changed. Snatching up clean clothes for the toddler, Katie proceeded to clean her up.

"I don't suppose there is any talking you out of this idea of yours?"

"No, ma'am. Please don't be unhappy with me. We won't be gone long, I promise. When I get back I'll bake the pies, and then we can spend the rest of the evening together." Katie saw Elizabeth smile.

"Katie, you bundle up warm, or you will be sick for your wedding day," Elizabeth cautioned. "And take my scarf; it's warmer."

❧

The sun shone down long enough to send the temperatures up a few degrees, and it felt warm on Peyton's and Katie's backs as they left Fort Davis. Peyton rode his bay mare and Katie rode her spotted horse. She hadn't ridden since coming to the fort, but Seth had made sure the animal had been exercised and properly groomed. Elizabeth fussed and scolded over Katie's choice of riding bareback, but it did little good. Elizabeth's parting words to Peyton warned him of his stubborn bride.

"Don't let those green eyes and angelic face fool you, Sergeant Sinclair. She will be a handful, mark my word. It's not too late for you to postpone the wedding and let me train her right for you," Elizabeth said, attempting to sound angry, but Katie saw right through it.

"I think you want to mother me a while longer," Katie said laughing.

Peyton promised to send her home on a regular basis for training, and Elizabeth appeared satisfied.

The two galloped out over the valley beyond Wild Rose Pass and across the prairie. Although the land looked brown and barren, Katie could easily imagine the green and color of spring. The wind whipped their faces, and Katie was glad Elizabeth had insisted upon a scarf. A quick glance back showed the fort clearly in the distance.

"Slow down, Katie," Peyton called to her.

"I'm enjoying my last day of freedom," Katie shouted back, but she did bring the horse to a trot.

"You will need to improve on taking orders," Peyton said, bringing the bay to her side. "This time tomorrow, Mrs. Peyton Sinclair will be expected to do her husband's bidding."

"And if I don't?" she asked, pretending insolence.

"The stockade. That's where all unruly wives learn military discipline," Peyton explained.

"It probably won't do a bit of good," Katie said. "What comes next?"

Peyton gave her a devilish grin. "I'll tell you tomorrow."

She felt herself blush and realized she had fallen into his wit once again.

Peyton leaned up against the saddle horn. "We may have company," he said casually.

"Who?" Katie asked, wondering who would be out riding in the cold.

Peyton slowed his horse to a walk, and Katie followed his lead. "I saw the Kiowa this morning. I made sure he knew our plans. So if he has a message from Lone Eagle, we will find out shortly."

"Oh, I don't think we have to worry," Katie said, looking for signs of the scout. "The wedding's tomorrow; Lone Eagle would have sent word by now. Surely he's forgotten about me and won't waste his time."

"I hope so," Peyton said, but she heard doubt lacing his words.

Katie's gaze met Peyton. She saw no useful purpose in lying. "I don't believe he has decided to leave me alone, either. But he's nearly run out of time."

"I agree, sweetheart." Peyton pulled his horse to a stop, and Katie did the same. "We ought to start back. The air's getting colder, and there's no sign of the Kiowa."

"Does anyone besides Colonel Ross and myself know you speak Comanche?" Katie asked quietly.

"No, and I don't intend for anyone to find out. Too many times it's helped me get out of trouble."

"Or into trouble," Katie said dryly.

"Well, that too."

The horses picked their way through the terrain toward Fort Davis, and Katie allowed Peyton's teasing to keep her mind from the Kiowa. She wanted to savor every minute alone with Peyton so she would always remember the afternoon of December 23, the day before their wedding.

A gust of northern wind blew a harsh chill against their faces. Katie shivered and realized a warm fire would feel very good.

"Are you thinking the Kiowa may not have a message for me?" She earnestly wanted Peyton to agree with her conclusion. The thought of Lone Eagle setting her free was a precious thought, even if it did sound like a fool's dream.

"Sweetheart, I've prayed for that very thing," Peyton said soberly. "I want it all to be over, just like you do—perhaps more so. I don't care how selfish it sounds, but our wedding needs to begin without any fear of Lone Eagle's influence in our lives. When we are married, I will relax."

"We haven't talked about it for several weeks," Katie said. "Once I worried he would make his demands after we were married, except. . .oh, never mind." Katie felt herself redden at her own thoughts.

"What, Katie?" Peyton saw her chagrin and shook his head. "This time tomorrow we will be husband and wife. I think you can tell me what's floating around in that blond head of yours."

Katie patted the neck of her spotted horse, then tightened the scarf around her neck. "I don't think Lone Eagle would want me after I had a husband," she managed to say. "Unless he intended to punish me."

"He won't have much time to plan anything of the sort. I still would like to head back to Illinois in the spring. He can't follow us there."

"True, and he's not about to let up on the raids. The Kiowa spoke true when he pointed out the Comanches wouldn't fight over a woman," Katie said, finally voicing her fears. "Pride and honor might send him after me, but nothing else. Lone Eagle won't give up until the army stops the whole Comanche nation."

"You can be certain of that," Peyton muttered. "The army will have to send reinforcements before any security is made in this territory, and. . .look up to the ridge, Katie!"

Katie fastened her gaze on a ridge to the west of them. The afternoon sun provided a backdrop to the party of over fifty Comanche warriors. She saw their horses prance, eager to run, and fear ripped through every part of her. Black war paint, the color of death, fairly glistened on their faces. Lone

Eagle's horse stepped out in full view.

Lone Eagle will kill Peyton for sure, she thought wildly. *Calm down and think!*

"What do we do?" Katie asked, not once taking her eyes from Lone Eagle. "They are far too close to the fort. Oh no, Lone Eagle is planning to attack while everyone is preparing for Christmas. Peyton, we're just in the way."

"We could run for it," Peyton said. He turned in the saddle to take a better view of the country around them. "We can't outrun these Comanches, Katie. There are another forty or fifty Comanches on the other side, and they are moving in around us. The Kiowa is behind this, I'm sure."

Katie focused her attention on Lone Eagle. "He can't see my fear," she whispered. "But I am afraid."

"Me, too, sweetheart. We fooled ourselves into believing our wedding would take place without problems from Lone Eagle. I really wanted to spend the rest of my life with you."

Katie nodded slightly. "I love you, Peyton, and I'm sorry to have brought you to this." She looked to the ridge again. "Perhaps I should try to talk to him."

Peyton interrupted her words. "Don't put your own life on the line for me. I'm a soldier, remember? We're supposed to be heroes." Peyton hesitated. "You know, I can't picture myself letting Lone Eagle take you from me without a fight. And we're close enough to the fort that rifle fire would warn the others of the attack. This bay has won a few races, and your horse is surefooted. I want to bet on outrunning them."

"I'm ready when you are," Katie whispered. "God be with you, Peyton, because Lone Eagle will try to kill you first."

seventeen

Katie silently cried out for more time. She needed to tell Peyton all those things dear to her heart—those words she'd savored for their wedding night. This was all her fault! She had been the one to insist upon riding so far from the fort; her own selfishness had gotten them into this death trap. Too many words were left unspoken, and she feared she would never have another chance to tell Peyton how much she loved him.

Dear God, I'm scared. Lone Eagle will kill Peyton for sure. I don't care what happens to me, but please watch over Peyton. He's the innocent one. I'm sorry for being so selfish and stubborn. It's my fault, and I know it. All Peyton has ever done is try to protect and love me. Oh God, he can't die because of me!

Peyton spurred his horse north, away from the trail toward the fort. Katie dug her heels into the sides of her horse and joined him. They raced side by side as the warriors sped down from the ridge. Comanche war cries echoed in every direction, and the foreboding screams urged her mount on faster. She leaned low against its neck just like Jeremiah had taught her and vowed not to look behind. It would only slow down the escape. Katie stole a glance at Peyton; he, too, bent over the bay's neck. Even with the weight of the saddle, the bay ran like a bolt of lightning. Their horses' pace made her think they might have a chance. Both animals lunged into the wind as though they sensed the impending danger. Every muscle was conditioned to respond to the rider, but so were the Comanche horses.

Peyton had led them north, and then he circled back south

around the ridge. The Comanches didn't expect him to head away from the fort, and their braves were concentrated on the south side. The warriors would have to race down the ridge and across the flat terrain to catch them. Katie heard the sound of advancing Indian horses pounding against the hard ground. The hooves hammered louder, and she knew Lone Eagle and his warriors were not far behind. Peyton's move had bought precious little time.

The crack of rifle fire broke into the chase. She smelled the pungent odor of sulfur, and heard the bullets whiz past her. Katie tensed; she *could* endure a rifle shot and not slow the horse's pace. A prayer flashed across her mind: *Dear Lord, please keep Peyton safe from Comanche fire, and don't let me slow him down.* She refused to be the cause of the Comanches overtaking her and Peyton. Determined to outrun the Indians, Katie didn't see the flesh rip away from Peyton's shoulder slightly above his previous wound. Her senses moved her to steal a look at him. The sight of blood and the anguish tearing across his face intensified the gravity of their situation. Fright blinded her from seeing anything but a vision of Peyton lying mutilated, like the bodies of the Lawrence family. He didn't dare allow the Comanches a chance to torture him.

Katie hurried her horse closer to the mare's side. Their mounts heaved heavily with the speed, and a sheen of sweat glittered from their sides. Peyton refused to look her way, but Katie saw a steady stream of blood soak his shoulder down to his wrist.

"Get out of here!" Peyton called. "Pull away from me!"

"No!" Katie cried against the piercing cold. "I won't leave you."

Her eyes fixed on the path ahead of them, and she could see several of the warriors moving around a patch of rock to position themselves in their path. It would only be a matter of moments before she and Peyton were overtaken. Only an angel of God could save them now. Silently she prayed death would come quickly to Peyton. Lone Eagle would make him pay greatly for her foolishness.

Katie remembered the times when she heard God's whisper calling for her to trust Him. *Have Peyton and my lives existed for this moment?* she asked herself. *Are we to die together, or will Lone Eagle force me to watch Peyton's slow torture? Lord, please save him from this.*

Another bullet tore away the lower skirt of her dress. For a moment, Katie wished the warrior's aim had ended the chase, then she quickly pushed the thought aside. She would not be known for inviting death as an easy way out.

Up ahead, something diverted the warriors' attention. Comanche braves scattered in different directions. What were they planning? The pursuing band clearly dispersed, providing a clear path ahead. Katie didn't understand their strategy; it seemed useless to ambush when they held her and Peyton in the midst of them.

Katie strained to hear a peculiar sound. Was that rifle fire to the front of them? In her delirium, could it be the Comanches' shots merely echoed in an endless circle? Katie squinted to see beyond the warriors. Were those images really riders headed this way? Could it be blue uniforms racing to meet them? Katie recognized the stance of one of the colonel's scouts. God had heard her prayers. Soldiers rode toward them at breakneck speed, firing straight into the Comanches. Katie saw two warriors drop and another lose his horse. *Praise God!* she wanted to shout. Taking a quick inspection of Peyton, she saw this hope gave him strength to continue on. *Just a little farther, Peyton. We're going to make it.*

Without warning, Katie felt the brush of an unseen rider. In the next instant, an arm snatched her from the horse's back. It happened too quickly for her to fight or scream; she had no warning. Katie's body flew suspended in the wind with only the arm of her captor balancing her between life and death. Terror numbed her senses as a scream rose and fell in her throat. Helpless, Katie watched her horse travel straight into the path of safety without her. In an instant, the warrior pulled her quivering body in front of him. He angled his horse away from the pursuing soldiers and raced toward the hills. She stared down at the scarred arm wrapped securely around her. Katie knew without a doubt that Lone Eagle held her captive.

The struggling proved useless. The more Katie fought against Lone Eagle, the tighter he pulled her body to his until the pressure against her stomach forced her to cry out. Consciousness escaped her as she fell prey to momentary blackness. How well she understood the plight of a snared animal, and visions of Jeremiah's traps tore across her mind. The agony of enraged animals would cower to pitiful whimpers from the pain of the trap's teeth. Death would be a welcomed in the face of hideous pain.

Each time Katie twisted or tried to peel away from Lone Eagle's arm, he gripped her waist and drew her body closer to him. She fell limp into periods of darkness where only her sense of sound prevailed with the steady labored panting of the animal beneath them.

The horse slowed to a gallop. . .a trot. . .then a walk. Wearily she fought the suffocating blackness. . .if only Lone Eagle would release his hold upon her. But didn't she want death? Wouldn't the grave be a warmer place than surrendering to the warrior?

"Would you like to live?" Lone Eagle whispered in her ear. His breath against her neck sickened her. Katie stiffened; his words brought her back from a haze.

The sound of Comanche words flooded her mind with memories. She recalled a little girl hanging onto Jeremiah's hand. Quickly the child transformed into a young woman. She held the hand of Lone Eagle and walked with him up a mountain path. What had happened? Pictures of the Lawrence family lying in grotesque positions in the back of their wagon flashed vividly before her. Lone Eagle's imperative question pressed against her senses, but she failed to reply. Katie didn't want to live, except the God who gave her life must be the One to take it.

"Would you like to live?" Lone Eagle repeated, and she heard anger clearly tip his words. He lifted a knife to her throat. The icy sharpness against her skin sealed any desire to die at his hand.

"Yes, I want to live," Katie said hoarsely.

"My wife will not run away?" Lone Eagle asked.

Katie felt the blade against her throat. "No, I will not run away."

"Two warriors die because of you," he spat, "but the white soldier is dead. He fell from his horse when hit by another bullet."

You are wrong, Katie replied to herself. She had seen Peyton ride straightway toward the soldiers. *He lives,* she silently screamed. *Peyton made it to safety; I know he did. Lone Eagle wants me to believe Peyton died. It is easier to keep me from running away if I have no one to return to. His deceit gives him victory, but I won't allow it. Lone Eagle may rule my future, but he will never rule my heart.*

Exhaustion played upon her body, and the cold cut through to her bones. Her stomach ached and cramped from the force of Lone Eagle's arm. Katie ignored the pain; she had to think. She had to pray.

Then suddenly the Comanche village came into view. Katie stretched her neck to see if anything had changed. It looked as peaceful as she remembered, but the Indians would most likely be unfriendly now that Lone Eagle had lost warriors in getting her back. She knew the plight of Comanche slaves; it would be a life worse than death. Men and women alike would beat and torture her for no other reason than to claim their superiority. Katie wished she knew the plans Lone Eagle had for her. He'd called her his wife—but in what fashion?

Lone Eagle slid down from the back of his horse. A crowd formed around the warriors. Some cheered at the one who had added another white man's scalp, and others looked sullen due to the deaths of the two men. Katie's appearance brought no reaction. Perhaps they thought she wanted to return to them.

Lone Eagle pulled her down from his horse. "Go to my teepee," he ordered.

Katie did not protest. What good would it do?

She waited inside until the need to relieve herself became too great. Her stomach hurt from Lone Eagle's rough treatment, and all she really wanted to do was sleep. No one stopped her outside the teepee, but she felt the eyes of everyone piercing through her.

Once again she waited until dusk.

Lone Eagle lifted the flap of the teepee and stepped inside. His presence filled the small dwelling, but she didn't feel his domination drawing her to him as in the past. Katie had prepared food for him; he would expect it of her. She took a deep breath and lifted her eyes warily to see his response.

A look of contempt and hostility challenged any rebellion she might have fostered. Lone Eagle's face looked hard and stoic. If Katie had wondered if the Comanche still held any feelings for her, the question vanished in a single glance.

"I have food for you," she said simply. Katie peered into his face, determined he would not see her fright.

A silent, angry stare served as a reply. Lone Eagle took a position near the food and began to eat. Katie hesitated, then kneeled beside him.

"Lone Eagle, I can't stay here with you tonight," Katie began.

His hand instantly flew to the side of her face, sending her sprawling to the side of him. She tasted the blood trickling from the corner of her mouth, but she did not cry out. It would only invite more of the same.

"Please let me explain," she continued. "It is my woman's time."

His hand raised to strike her again, but Katie buried her face in her hands.

"You liar," he said low. "Tomorrow you were to marry the white soldier."

"A woman doesn't always know about such things," she said, feeling the warm flush of humiliation.

"If you lie, I will peel the flesh from your bones," Lone Eagle threatened.

"I am telling you the truth," Katie maintained.

"Get out of my teepee until your time is over."

eighteen

Katie followed the familiar path to Desert Fawn's teepee. Their relationship began when Katie first came to the village. After Mary Colter's death, Jeremiah entrusted Katie to Desert Fawn's care. He could not be consoled, neither could he care for the child properly. The Indian woman sheltered and nurtured Katie in those early years, and the little girl soon attached herself to the old woman. Katie called her grandmother, and the two formed a bond of love and companionship. Now she wondered how the old woman would receive Lone Eagle's captive.

Katie understood Jeremiah's intense grief over losing his wife and infant son. The couple had put their mistakes behind them to build and share a future together. In Jeremiah's mind, he had lost everything he treasured. By burying Mary's Bible, he marked his desperate rebellion against God. For a time, it looked as though Jeremiah had gone mad, especially when he left Katie with Desert Fawn and took to the mountains. Upon his return, Jeremiah Colter adopted the Comanche ways. He passed the test of a warrior by proving himself in battle and earned a title of distinction when he saved Swift Arrow's life. Katie did not ask how he obtained the title of a warrior, nor did she want to know.

Jeremiah abandoned and seemingly forgot the customs of his own people. He loved his little girl, but he devoted more time to the traditions and culture of the Indians. She saw her father cast aside the practices of the white man, and take on all of the characteristics of a warrior. During this significant transition in Jeremiah's life, Katie learned many lessons about Indian life from Desert Fawn. If not for Comanche children

149

teasing her about the color of her skin and hair, she would have forgotten her white heritage.

As Katie deliberated upon those days, she realized the biggest difference in Jeremiah's and her life lay in how they reacted to tragedy. Jeremiah turned from God when her mother died, and she drew closer to God when he died. Katie would not be disillusioned over the Creator of the world.

Confusion mixed with gratitude met Katie's senses as she pondered over her unexpected woman's time. Never had she considered it a blessing, but it did provide a few more days of freedom before Lone Eagle claimed her. Not that it changed the inevitable, except she could spend the days in prayer for strength and grace to endure the future. Comanche culture demanded she not sleep in her husband's teepee during these days. It also stated she could not eat meat, comb her hair, or wash her face. Before Katie resumed normal activity with her husband, culture demanded she bathe in the icy river.

Perhaps God intends to better prepare me for the role of Lone Eagle's wife, she thought. *Oh God, please speak to me. I can't fulfill my responsibilities to Lone Eagle alone. He's so angry, and according to his customs, he has a right to punish me however he wishes. Help me to accept what You plan for my life and to be content in all circumstances.*

Different Scriptures came to mind. She could recall the words but not always the books, chapters, and numbers of the verses. Katie thanked God for His Word stored in her heart.

Katie stopped in front of Desert Fawn's teepee. Trepidation halted her steps. Had Lone Eagle expressed his anger and distrust to everyone in the village? Would the grandmother she loved now be turned against her?

Katie hesitantly opened the flap of Desert Fawn's teepee. The old woman labored over a pair of winter boots made from buffalo hides. Katie watched her roll moistened sinew on her knee until it formed a point and could be threaded through a bone needle. Desert Fawn had made many pairs of winter footwear and beaded moccasins for Katie. As a child, she had watched the old woman sew garments, and her skill still fascinated Katie.

"Desert Fawn," Katie whispered.

The old woman turned in disbelief, and with open arms they reached for each other and shed quiet tears. Katie fondly remembered Desert Fawn's many wrinkles, and the leathery hand still stroked her hair as though she was a child again.

"I've missed you," Katie finally said, and she thanked God for someone who loved her when life seemed torn apart.

"Why are you here, little one?" the old woman asked.

Katie didn't know how to tell her without showing disrespect for Lone Eagle. "Lone Eagle brought me," she replied simply.

Desert Fawn merely nodded. She knew the truth.

"Can I stay with you for a few days?" Katie asked. "It is my woman's time."

The old woman smiled. "Sit by the fire with me. You can watch me stitch moccasins like you were a child again."

God had granted Katie peace for a little while.

The following day would have been her wedding day. Katie tried to center her thoughts on the meaning of Christmas and not the ugliness separating her from Peyton, but it didn't stop the continuous lump in her throat.

The next two days passed quickly. One of Desert Fawn's sons invited them to follow a buffalo hunt, and the two trailed behind with the other women. When the warrior had killed the animal, she and Katie skinned it, dressed the meat, and packed it on a pony to return to camp.

"It seems like a long time since we have prepared buffalo for winter," Katie said. "You always work faster than me at jerking out the pieces. My fingers are weak, and yours are swift and strong."

The old woman smiled and Katie watched the sun glisten off her silver hair.

"When you are as old as I am, then you, too, can work faster," Desert Fawn said.

"Yes, but you are the best teacher. Look, we will finish pulling the meat apart today. Tomorrow it can lie in the sun."

"And the next day we can slice it into thin strips so it can harden. My teepee will have plenty of meat during the winter," Desert Fawn boasted.

Desert Fawn and Katie reminisced about the past and repeated stories about Katie as a child. Katie did not mention life at Fort Davis; she should forget all of it. The two laughed and talked; they mourned Jeremiah and cried.

"Lone Eagle is a brave warrior," Desert Fawn said. "He is fearless in leading warriors against the whites. Jeremiah should not have told you to return to them. You could have died with all the whites."

Katie felt the familiar churning in her stomach. "Yes, Lone Eagle is a brave warrior."

"Are you now afraid of him?" the old woman asked.

"A woman should always fear her husband," Katie replied, and nothing more was said.

That evening as the two sat around the fire warming themselves, Katie felt an urgency to talk to Desert Fawn about God.

"I have learned many things about the Great Spirit," Katie said. "Not the god of the sun, mother earth, or the moon, but the one and only Great Spirit."

Desert Fawn looked confused, but she leaned closer to hear Katie's words.

"The Great Spirit loves all of us, and He wants us to live in peace. He loves us so much that He sent His only Son to teach us the ways of love and how to live in peace. The people of earth did not want to learn these things. They wanted to be warriors and grew angry with the Great Spirit's Son. They plotted and killed Him, but they did not know the Great Spirit had planned for His Son to die for their evil ways. After three

days, the Great Spirit raised His Son from the dead to show
all people of His love and power. The Great Spirit said all
who believe My Son died and rose again to life will live with
Me forever."

"Ah, the *Habbe Weich-ket* death song." The old woman
began to sing softly. "How great his people were. How great a
patriot he was. How he loved his country and his people.
How he fought for them with no thought of the Happy
Hunting Ground until his people thought of it for him."

Katie felt Desert Fawn understood a little of what she was
trying to explain. Comanches did not concern themselves
about death until it happened. It would take more than one
meeting for her dear friend to understand the Almighty God,
and the thought of peace among the Indians would crumble
the strongest Comanche. Katie wished she had her Bible. Her
own instructions had barely begun, and there were many
things she didn't know or understand.

The day of her ritual bathing came. Unlike the previous
days of bleak, gray clouds, the sun shone warm and shim-
mered upon the water. Katie stepped into the cold river. Its
frigid temperatures took her breath away, and she felt certain
her heart stopped beating. For a moment Katie considered the
irony of catching pneumonia and facing death like Jeremiah.
Would she prefer death to marriage to Lone Eagle?

Wrapped in a thick blanket, Katie sat upon the riverbank
and watched the ripples break out across the water. It felt
strange to be clothed in the pale yellow deerskin again, and
the winter boots lined with buffalo fur warmed her icy toes.
Yet the softness and scent of her Comanche clothes brought
back a happier time when she shared a teepee with Jeremiah
and Desert Fawn.

Katie used her fingers to comb through the wet tresses,
then she braided her hair in one long braid. Her thoughts
drifted to those near to her heart and especially for those she
would never see again.

I don't want to be an emotionless woman, Katie told herself. *If my life is to be here, then I must find joy in small things. I must do everything possible to be a good wife to Lone Eagle—not just cook and do chores or bear his children but devote my life to making his days happy. I don't have to agree with what he does or dwell upon what could have been with Peyton. God walks with me, and I'm not alone.*

Taking a deep breath, Katie reluctantly stood. The day would proceed as planned with or without her approval. She needed to collect firewood and prepare food for Lone Eagle's evening meal. Katie dared not delay in returning to Lone Eagle's teepee. It made little sense to anger him.

Suddenly she sensed someone's presence. It sent chills up her spine to think a warrior had watched while she bathed. She turned to see a familiar figure standing in the brush behind her.

"Lone Eagle," Katie said. "I didn't see you."

The Comanche strode alongside her. "I haven't been here long. Desert Fawn told me you were at the river."

"I am returning to your teepee today," Katie said simply. She observed him closely for signs of hostility, but he appeared calm.

Lone Eagle nodded and his gaze passed by her and onto the river.

Katie hesitated before speaking, but she felt compelled to put her thoughts into words. "I meant what I said to you before—I'll never try to leave you, and I will do my best to be a good wife."

His gaze rested upon her face. It took all of her courage to stare into his ebony eyes, but she feared condemnation by avoiding him. Better she show bravery than shy away like a coward.

"Sit beside me," he said. "We haven't talked for many months."

Obediently, Katie shifted the blanket around her and

resumed her position on the riverbank. Her heart beat so fiercely that she felt certain he heard it pounding.

"I never thought you wouldn't want to come back," Lone Eagle began. "And I never thought I would see fear in your eyes. The white man has turned you against the Comanche, for now you see me as the enemy."

Katie said nothing because she rejected the urge to lie. Lone Eagle would read the deceit and despise her for it.

"While I waited, you chose a white soldier to take my place. You planned to have two husbands," he said bitterly. "My anger against you and all the whites could not be satisfied. I wanted you dead; I wanted to cut out your heart for what you had done to me."

Lone Eagle sat silent and motionless. Katie heard the pace of his breathing; she'd provoked his temper.

"My father told me about your promise to Jeremiah, but it didn't matter," Lone Eagle continued. "He had accepted the gifts of many fine horses. Why did he ask you to leave?"

His words were demanding, and Katie's refusal to answer the warrior only invited punishment.

"I didn't know then, either," Katie said. She breathed a prayer and God calmed her trembling. "It took some time for me to understand and accept what he wanted for me. Please believe me when I say I didn't want to leave here. My heart belonged to you and no one else. I wanted the people at the fort to send me away—back to you. Instead, Jeremiah's brother and his wife welcomed me into their home. They loved and took care of me. Neither one of them criticized me for living among the Comanches. They accepted me as one of their own."

"You are Jeremiah Colter's daughter and Lone Eagle's wife, a Comanche," he stated with deadly seriousness.

Katie sighed heavily. "No, I am not Jeremiah Colter's daughter."

She felt Lone Eagle's eyes upon her, piercing and angry.

"I found out Jeremiah Colter wasn't my father; his brother is my real father. I'm certain that is why he made me promise to return to Fort Davis. He wanted me to be with my true father."

"And you did not know about this?" Lone Eagle demanded.

"No," Katie whispered. "It was very difficult for me to hear those words and forgive them."

"Is this why you agreed to marry the white soldier?" Lone Eagle asked.

Katie thought how easy it would be to lie and save herself. Lone Eagle could very well be sympathetic to her if he thought she agreed to marry Peyton out of unhappiness. Her reply determined her future, her life. It looked tempting. . .

"No, I agreed to marry before I found out about my parents."

She felt him stiffen and braced herself for him to strike her.

Lone Eagle appeared to ponder her words. "You could have lied to me," he said. "You know the penalty for an unfaithful wife."

"I did not consider myself your wife because we had not lived together. I knew what it meant when Jeremiah accepted your gifts, but I returned them to you."

"I thought differently," Lone Eagle said.

Katie knew the price an adulteress paid. Lone Eagle could have her killed, mutilated, or the tip of her nose cut off. He could do anything because she was his chattel. Her hope lay in the fact he owned her. Would Lone Eagle want to destroy his own property? The answer came from the many past deliberations about her relationship with the Comanche warrior. He had to maintain his pride and honor among the tribe. The other Comanches respected his position, but it was up to Lone Eagle to keep it.

Katie didn't like surprises; she desperately needed to know the warrior's intentions. Lone Eagle must have decided her fate, or he wouldn't have sought her out.

"What are you going to do with me?" Katie asked. She again fought the trembling in her body and wondered if he planned to punish her there by the river.

Lone Eagle's hardened features told her nothing. His eyes stayed fixed on the water gurgling peacefully. The warrior stood, and she instantly rose beside him.

"I want to kill you," Lone Eagle said, glaring straight into her eyes. "Every white man, woman, and child I killed held your face. Their screams became your screams. Their blood became your blood. I watched them suffer through torture after torture, wishing they were you. Do you think I want you to live?"

nineteen

The sun parted the clouds of winter and seemingly mocked Katie's anxiety as she viewed its slow descent. The hours moved by swiftly, yet not quickly enough. Let the evening come soon but not too soon. Confusion twisted and turned her thoughts and emotions. Terror danced across Katie's mind as though Lone Eagle's hatred could be crushed into meaningless threats. Agonizing turmoil erupted again, pushing her further into a state of panic. Hopelessness. Reality.

If Lone Eagle planned to kill her through some hideous torture, then why had he waited to make it known? Did his satisfaction come in devising the torture to make her pay for leaving him? Stories about mutilated victims repeated until each accounting sounded like the last, and all the tales rolled into one. Visions of the Lawrence family focused before her eyes. The scent of blood-soaked bodies filled the air, and she knew not where the stench came from. Cries of terror echoed all around, calling out her name to join the spirits of the dead, and she tasted bile from her own vomit.

Waiting produced its own gruesome nightmare.

Katie hugged Desert Fawn close to her and said good-bye. The old woman asked her to visit often, and Katie agreed. She couldn't tell this precious woman of Lone Eagle's words. Desert Fawn could do nothing, and Katie refused to alarm her.

As she expected, Lone Eagle's teepee stood cold and empty. He had not said when he would be returning, and she feared too much to ask. Gathering firewood and preparing food for Lone Eagle kept her hands busy but not her mind.

Katie's thoughts drifted back to a time soon after her

mother's death. She and Jeremiah had worked since sunup packing their belongings for the journey to the Comanche village. As Jeremiah sorted through the last of the things they needed, Katie ventured into the garden to search for any remaining vegetables. She'd finished one row and started another when the distinct hissing of a rattler met her ears. Panic seized the little girl's body, and she couldn't move or speak. Katie held onto a cornstalk, frozen, and watched the snake coil and poise to strike. In the flash of an instant, a knife pierced the rattler's head, ending its deadly mission. Jeremiah grabbed the little girl and held her close. He trembled and held her as tightly as though once more he kneeled at Mary's grave.

"How did you know to come, Pa?" Katie asked.

Jeremiah looked at her strangely. "I heard you call for help, child."

"No, Pa. I was too scared to talk or move."

Jeremiah looked deeply into her green eyes and shook his head, incredulous of what had happened.

Katie felt the familiar tug at her heart, missing Jeremiah. He couldn't protect her now; no one could. Katie brushed aside the recollection. Like so many times in the last days, her faith wavered. Unbelief whispered taunting words to a mind desperately needing something to grasp. Her senses became cold and numb, yet did she hear a faint whisper?

Trust Me, Katie.

❧

Evening shadows had stolen away the reflections of late afternoon when Lone Eagle arrived at the teepee. Wordlessly he peered down at her with no expression of anger or hatred. Katie met his scrutiny by challenging him with her own unemotional stare. Once, her greatest fear of Lone Eagle rested on living the rest of her life as his wife. That same fear became her one hope when he disclosed his passion to kill her. Now she waited for him to choose in which manner she should die.

He moved with confidence and power, reminding her of a mountain cat cautiously picking its way across a canyon wall. Beneath his heavy buffalo robe dwelled a mass of defined muscle and trained nerves ever alert to kill at a moment's notice. Katie wanted to deny any memories of loving this man, but lies did not become her. Even at this moment fear took precedence over hatred. He removed the robe and sat beside the fire. Katie sat back from the blaze while he ate the quail, pecans, and dried berries she had roasted for him.

Odd and peculiar thoughts floated through her mind as she focused her attention on a burning log. Why hadn't she used a knife on herself? Ultimately, she would have denied him the pleasure of watching her die. Weary of the waiting and anxious to be free of the unknown, she felt a surge of courage to step into the black haze of his mind.

Katie breathed a quick prayer. "What are you going to do with me?" she asked.

His whole body appeared to respond to her words. He placed the food on the dirt floor and pulled out his knife. It glittered wickedly in the firelight, and she asked herself how many other victims fell under his blade.

"Why do you not fear me?" Lone Eagle asked bitterly, turning the knife over in his hand.

"I am afraid," Katie admitted. "But in death there is life."

"Your words make no sense," he shot at her.

"I have a God who will take my spirit with Him to live forever," she said quietly. "I cannot fight you; I cannot resist you. I can only draw strength from my God to endure whatever you choose to do."

"You speak white man's words!"

"No. These words are for all people. God loves us all and longs to save us all from the evil in our hearts."

Lone Eagle shoved her against the dirt floor. He jumped to his feet and threw the knife, snaring the sleeve of her dress to the ground. Lone Eagle turned and stormed from the teepee.

Katie pulled the knife from her sleeve. Bewildered by Lone Eagle's actions, she laid the weapon by his unfinished food. *He wants to kill me, but something is stopping him. Has he enjoyed the hunt for so long that my capture is disappointing? How long will this go on?*

Long after the village rested quietly and the sounds of darkness cradled the night creatures, Katie listened for Lone Eagle to return. Exhausted, she lay beneath the buffalo robes too tired to weep or think. Her body relaxed and she slept.

Katie woke with the early morning sounds of singing birds and busy insects. A faint trickle of dawn filtered in through the teepee opening, and she smelled the aroma of a freshly built fire. *Lone Eagle returned and didn't waken me,* Katie thought. *God has delivered me one more time from certain death.*

When Katie reflected upon the last week, God had protected her since Lone Eagle pulled her from the racing horse.

Her gaze rested upon the place where she had set Lone Eagle's knife. It was gone as well as the food. Katie didn't understand the warrior's behavior, but before she could further deliberate on all of the unusual happenings since Lone Eagle brought her to the village, he stepped inside.

"We're leaving," Lone Eagle announced. "The horses are ready."

Katie instantly obeyed. With a hint of sleep still dulling her senses, she wrapped a buffalo robe around her and followed him outside. The air felt cold and crisp against her face, serving to alert her senses to the early morning confusion.

Within moments the two rode from the Comanche village and headed south. At one point, Katie almost asked Lone Eagle where they were going, except she thought better of it. The warrior would unfold his plans as he saw fit, and she didn't want to displease him.

Under any other circumstances, Katie would have reveled in the beauty of sunrise. Behind a backdrop of towering mountains, the sun emerged, pulling purple and orange banners from a navy blue sky. She smiled at the scene spreading color and light to a sleepy world. Katie felt Lone Eagle's gaze studying her, but she ignored him. Best now she pray and concern herself with him later.

The two stopped beside a narrow stream to refresh themselves and their horses. Katie kneeled beside the water and cupped her hands to drink. She hadn't eaten the day before, and the cool water helped fill the gnawing in her stomach. Again she felt Lone Eagle staring at her. This time she took a deep breath and boldly met his ebony eyes. Perhaps it was the serenity of a new day or the knowledge they were the only two people for miles around, but Katie saw a trace of tenderness. It shocked her, yet in an instant she understood Lone Eagle's unrest. That quickly, he concealed his vulnerability and ordered her back on the spotted horse.

They rode another hour until Katie saw the ridge where she and Peyton first viewed the Comanche warriors. What was Lone Eagle planning?

He brought his horse to a halt, and she did also.

"You can ride the rest of the way by yourself," he said.

"Are you letting me go?" Katie asked, afraid to believe her ears.

"Yes. I owe Jeremiah Colter this one favor, even if you are not his daughter. I still want to kill you, but the spirits won't let me. I've been tormented since this place." Lone Eagle pointed to the land around them. "You are my wife and my enemy, and I will free you this one time to return to your people and the white soldier."

Katie wanted to explain to Lone Eagle that it was God who interrupted his plans, but she couldn't bring herself to tell him.

"Lone Eagle, we aren't enemies. Two people who loved each other can't be enemies."

"You don't know the ways of men and war," he said coldly. "I will never spare you again; now go."

Katie felt the need to say more, but she chose to heed his words and urged the horse south toward Fort Davis.

The sun played in and out of the clouds, first bringing light and warmth, then casting a dismal shade of gray. Katie paid no mind to the weather because her heart and mind sang praises to the God who delivered her. When she reflected upon the miracles since her abduction, they brought tears to her eyes. She wondered how many others had been praying for her. She asked for forgiveness in doubting Him and not having the courage to tell Lone Eagle who had stopped him from killing her.

Peyton was alive! Lone Eagle told her to return to the white soldier. He hadn't been killed but had ridden to safety among the soldiers. Had Peyton believed she died also? What would he feel now that she'd been set free? After a week's time, he might not welcome her as before. He might think the worst. Katie shuddered once more, contemplating the hideous tortures Lone Eagle could have inflicted. But he hadn't, and to some folks her unharmed body indicated she had submitted to other things. *Let them think whatever they want,* she thought fiercely. *I know the truth.* The only persons who deserved to know what happened were Peyton, Seth, and Elizabeth, and she planned to tell them everything.

Lone Eagle. . .he admitted to being tormented by spirits since the afternoon with Peyton. The warrior tasted defeat by a power he didn't know existed. Katie remembered the hatred in his eyes and the bitterness in his voice. Lone Eagle wanted to kill her for the humiliation she had caused. He had administered immense suffering and slow agonizing torment, but he stood defenseless before a mighty God.

For an instant, Katie had seen a flicker of the warrior she once loved. Pity ruled her heart for he forced himself to deny any feelings of caring or compassion. Fortunately Katie read more in his eyes than he could ever confess. Perhaps Desert Fawn would tell him about God.

Katie squinted and viewed an outline of Fort Davis. She focused her attention on Black Mountain and Wild Rose Pass. Such a refuge for those who needed a haven in the midst of a troubled territory. She clearly recognized the cultural differences between her own people and the Indian. In many ways, the battle over the land was unfair. For as many Indians who vowed to rid the territory of the whites, there were hundreds and thousands more whites to come. The weaker would concede to slaughter and be driven from their homes, and Katie realized the Indian had the most to lose.

Jeremiah Colter had permitted Katie to see both worlds. He left a legacy of love and compassion to a child he loved as his own. He wanted Katie to find her rehoboth, a well of blessings and peace in a place provided by God. Katie couldn't have asked for more from any father.

A sensation of being watched or followed met Katie's senses. She tugged at the horse and paused to look around. Several feet behind her she surveyed the figure of Lone Eagle sitting proud and erect upon his horse. Katie realized she would never fully understand the Comanche warrior. She lifted her hand and waved good-bye.

twenty

A soldier searched the canyon walls surrounding Fort Davis. When satisfied no Indians had scaled its walls, he looked out over the valley. The soldier believed he saw the outline of a figure riding toward them. Folks were jumpy and irritable with the Comanches raiding and murdering every chance they took. He didn't want to be accused of not doing his job. He peered through his binoculars before calling attention to his superior.

"Sergeant Sinclair," the soldier called.

Peyton looked up from his position below. "Yes, soldier."

"Rider headin' this way, sir. Can't make out who it is."

"One of the scouts?" Peyton asked, rising to his feet. He winced, momentarily forgetting his wound. The shoulder no longer throbbed, but it did ache now and then.

"No, sir. It's an Indian. . .no, it's a white woman dressed in Indian clothes."

"Open the gate," Peyton shouted, hurrying toward the fort's entrance.

"What if it's a trap?" the soldier asked.

Peyton smiled broadly. "Then I welcome it."

Clutching his wounded shoulder, Peyton rushed through the gate. The pounding of his boots against the earth started a throb up and down his arm, but the pain would not hold him back. It had to be Katie, no one else could fit that description. Once he saw the blond hair around her shoulders, he began to run. He felt tears of relief and joy sting his eyes. Katie was alive and nothing else mattered to him.

Her horse broke into a slow gallop until it reached his side. Katie slid to the ground, crying and calling his name. Peyton instantly saw the purple bruise on the side of her face. He reached to touch it gingerly as though she might break.

"Are you all right?" Peyton asked anxiously.

Katie smiled through her own tears. "Yes, I'm fine. He didn't hurt me, Peyton, only my face. He wanted to—Lone Eagle wanted to kill me, but he couldn't. God stopped him, and Lone Eagle sent me back to you."

Again Peyton searched her face and slipped his fingers through her hair. "God brought you back to me," he whispered and drew her close until his lips touched hers.

❧

"Are you ready, Katie child?" Seth called.

Katie emerged from the evening shadows of Seth and Elizabeth's room, where she had dressed for the wedding. A smile spread across Seth's face.

"You take my breath away," he said gently. "You are your mother, Katherine Grace Colter, a beautiful angel. I hope Peyton realizes how precious you are to me."

"Oh, Papa," Katie lifted her face to plant a kiss on his cheek. "I love you so very much."

Elizabeth dabbed her eyes with a lace handkerchief. She reached to Katie's shoulder and adjusted a row of pearls.

"My wedding dress is so beautiful," Katie whispered through sparkling eyes. "Thank you for everything you've done." She gracefully touched the ivory satin gown that hugged her slender waist and flared to the floor.

"Hannah and Mary both wore it, and someday your own daughter will wear it on her wedding day," Elizabeth said. "And I have something else for you. Since you decided to wear your hair down, I thought you might like this." Elizabeth placed a wreath of dried wild roses into Katie's hand.

"It's so lovely," Katie said and swallowed her tears, "and so perfect. When did you make this?"

Elizabeth laughed. "Katie, you have been so busy with the wedding that it was really quite simple. Now, I'm not finished.

I know you wanted to carry your Bible, so I decorated it for you."

Seth handed Katie her Bible adorned with additional dried roses and white ribbons nestled in a crocheted doily.

Katie held her breath. "I don't know what to say."

"Thank you will do just fine," Elizabeth said, obviously pleased with Katie's response.

"I look so grand. Oh, do put the wreath in my hair," Katie urged.

Elizabeth fastened the rose wreath with two hairpins and stood back to admire the bride. "Let me give you one last hug before you become Mrs. Peyton Sinclair," she said.

As Elizabeth embraced Katie, the young woman once more realized how God had blessed her life. He'd performed one miracle after another, and she knew no end to her joy.

Seth placed Katie's coat around her shoulders and fastened the first button. "I can't have my little girl taking cold, now can I?" he asked fondly. He stood back and gave her one last look before reaching out to link his daughter's arm into his. "God has blessed me richly to see you marry. Let's not keep Peyton waiting any longer."

In the twilight shadows Katie saw the many people waiting outside the small church. She instantly realized they were dear friends who had come to see Sergeant Peyton Sinclair wed Katie Colter. A nervous twinge tickled her stomach as she smiled and nodded at those watching her pass by. Already there were voices from inside the church, indicating that it was full. Stepping into the doorway, she slipped off her coat and handed it to Elizabeth.

"I want Peyton to see me without this," she whispered. Smiling from her heart to her face, Katie caught a glimpse of the room where she would become Mrs. Peyton Sinclair. "Oh my," she said, trembling. "Everything is so beautiful."

Candles flickered in metal braces hung from wooden poles and lining both sides of the center aisle and the sides of the church. Dried wild rose bouquets were gathered with white ribbons and tied to candlesticks at the front of the church.

"I'm not worthy of this," she whispered. "Papa, I've never done a thing to deserve such a beautiful wedding."

Seth patted her hand. "Yes, you have, child," he whispered. "If I name them all, then I'll cry like Elizabeth."

Katie watched Peyton enter through the side door of the church and take his place alongside Reverend Cooper. She could see the smile upon his lips, and it lifted her heart.

A soldier began to play his fiddle—a soft, sweet tune unknown to Katie. Slowly she and Seth walked down front to greet Reverend Cooper and Peyton.

The Reverend opened his Bible.

"Heavenly Father, as You have ordained marriage as a holy estate, we humbly ask Your blessings upon this man and this woman as they stand before You to pledge their love. As You have commanded, a man shall leave his father and mother and cling to his wife, and they shall be one flesh.

"Into this holy estate this man and this woman come now to be united. If anyone, therefore, can show just cause why they may not be lawfully joined together, let him now speak, or forever hold his peace."

Reverend Cooper paused, looked out over the crowd and smiled. He turned to Peyton.

"Wilt thou have this woman to thy wedded wife, to live together after God's ordinance in the holy estate of matrimony? Wilt thou love her, comfort her, honor and keep her in sickness and in health, and, forsaking all others, keep thee only unto her, so long as ye both shall live?"

Peyton's voice boomed over the quiet crowd. "I will."

Thank You, Lord, for delivering me unto You, and for this man, Katie prayed.

Reverend Cooper gave Katie his attention.

"Wilt thou have this man to thy wedded husband, to live together after God's ordinance in the holy estate of matrimony?

Wilt thou love him, comfort him, honor and keep him in sickness and in health, and, forsaking all others, keep thee unto him, so long as ye both shall live?"

Katie wanted to shout, but her voice failed her. "I will," she whispered.

"Who giveth this woman to be married to this man?"

"Her father," Seth said proudly. Stepping back, he placed Katie's right hand into Peyton's and gave her one last kiss on her cheek.

Katie felt the firm grasp of Peyton's hand and his gentle squeeze. She turned to smile with jade green eyes meeting warm gray pools of endless love. Reverend Cooper's voice boomed out over the crowd as he read God's directions for a Christ-centered marriage.

As Peyton repeated his vows, she clung to every word, determined to remember the sound of his promise forever.

When Katie's turn came, emotion laced her voice, and she struggled to keep the tears from trickling down her face. Her hand trembled as Peyton slipped a gold band on her finger.

"God Almighty send you His light and truth to keep you all the days of your life. The hand of God protect you; His holy angels accompany you. May the Lord cause His grace to be mighty upon you. Amen.

"I now pronounce you husband and wife," the reverend said. "Peyton, you may kiss your bride."

ະ

Colonel Ross walked outside his office with Peyton. He extended his hand to the young man before him.

"Well, you are officially a civilian now," the colonel said. "I wish I could convince you to stay. The army needs good men like you."

"Thanks, Colonel, but I'm heading home to Illinois. Katie has everything packed and we're leaving with the supply wagons in the morning. I'm mighty grateful for the army escort."

"Glad to help. You take care of yourself and that fine wife of yours," the colonel said. "What are your plans?"

"I'm planning to finish medical school," Peyton said. "A few years back I wanted nothing to do with it, but times change. Now that I'm going to be a father, I want the best for my family."

Colonel Ross grinned. "I'm expecting you and Katie to write when the baby is born."

"Most certainly. You will probably hear me shouting all the way from Illinois."

Katie Sinclair watched her husband walk away from Colonel Ross, his discharge papers in hand. *God is good,* she told herself. *He gave me life, a Spirit of Truth, a loving husband, and my rehoboth.*

A Letter To Our Readers

Dear Reader:

In order that we might better contribute to your reading enjoyment, we would appreciate your taking a few minutes to respond to the following questions. When completed, please return to the following:

Rebecca Germany, Managing Editor
Heartsong Presents
PO Box 719
Uhrichsville, Ohio 44683

1. Did you enjoy reading *Rehoboth?*
   ❑ Very much. I would like to see more books
      by this author!
   ❑ Moderately
      I would have enjoyed it more if _____

      _____

2. Are you a member of **Heartsong Presents**? ❑Yes ❑No
   If no, where did you purchase this book?_____

   _____

3. What influenced your decision to purchase this
   book? (Check those that apply.)

   ❑ Cover   ❑ Back cover copy

   ❑ Title   ❑ Friends

   ❑ Publicity   ❑ Other_____

4. How would you rate, on a scale from 1 (poor) to 5
   (superior), the cover design? _____

5. On a scale from 1 (poor) to 10 (superior), please rate the following elements.

___Heroine   ___Plot

___Hero   ___Inspirational theme

___Setting   ___Secondary characters

6. What settings would you like to see covered in **Heartsong Presents** books?_____

_____

_____

7. What are some inspirational themes you would like to see treated in future books?_____

_____

_____

8. Would you be interested in reading other **Heartsong Presents** titles? ❏ Yes   ❏ No

9. Please check your age range:
   ❏ Under 18   ❏ 18-24   ❏ 25-34
   ❏ 35-45   ❏ 46-55   ❏ Over 55

10. How many hours per week do you read? _____

Name _____

Occupation _____

Address _____

City_____ State_____ Zip_____

Only You

*A Romantic Collection
of Inspirational Novellas*

Valentine's Day—a day of love, romance, and dreams. *Only You,* a collection of four all-new contemporary novellas from **Heartsong Presents** authors, will be available in January 1998. What better way to celebrate than with this collection written especially for Valentine's Day. Authors Sally Laity, Loree Lough, Debra White Smith, and Kathleen Yapp have practically become household names to legions of romance readers and this collection includes their photos and biographies.

(352 pages, Paperbound, 5" x 8")

·····Hearts♥ng·····

········ Presents ········

Great Inspirational Romance at a Great Price!

Heartsong Presents books are inspirational romances in contemporary and historical settings, designed to give you an enjoyable, spirit-lifting reading experience. You can choose wonderfully written titles from some of today's best authors like Peggy Darty, Sally Laity, Tracie Peterson, Colleen L. Reece, Lauraine Snelling, and many others.

When ordering quantities less than twelve, above titles are $2.95 each.
Not all titles may be available at time of order.